For
Eda Smith,
    with best wishes from her
South Berwick neighbor,
            Gladys Hasty Carroll

Nov. 15, 1950

Christmas Without Johnny

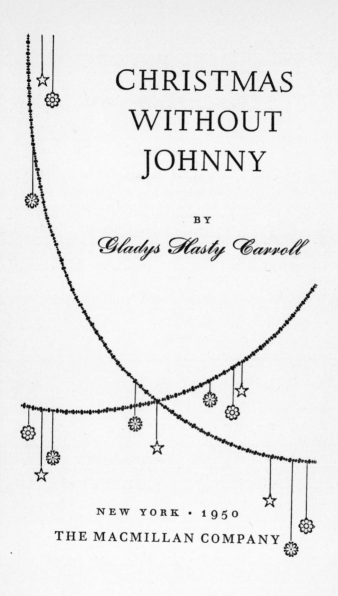

CHRISTMAS
WITHOUT
JOHNNY

BY

Gladys Hasty Carroll

NEW YORK · 1950

THE MACMILLAN COMPANY

Dedicated

with profound respect

to

ALICE B. ALLEN

a Maine grade-school teacher
whose lifelong devotion to children and whose
friendly, intelligent, creative relationship with them
sets an example to the nation

Contents

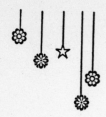

Friday

1

How long is it 'til Christmas?" Johnny asked in a low voice.

His mother turned from the stove to look at him, sitting alone at the kitchen table.

He was too small for a nine-year-old, she thought as she had a thousand times. The baby, Deirdre, took after Jack; Deir had long legs, broad shoulders and stout hands already; but Johnny was small-boned like herself. What a pity it should be that way! He was thin, too, as Marge had never been. She knew that was because he did not eat enough. His eyes were enormous. Where did he get such big eyes? Perhaps they only seemed so because his face was small.

She put a steaming bowl before him and stuck a spoon into it.

"Goodness, I don't know," she said. "I've been too busy to think. Now eat that up, son. Every bit. And keep your eye out for the bus.

I've got to run upstairs and strip the beds before Deir wakes up. Your lunch is on the chair by the door."

On her way she glanced at the calendar and paused.

Christmas . . . When she was nine, she had counted the days. Once she had crossed off each one before she went to bed, beginning at Thanksgiving. That was the last year she had wanted a doll. A doll with real hair which she could wash and curl. She had that doll still, and was keeping her for Deir.

"Why, it's only ten days," she said. "That isn't long, is it, Johnny? What you wishing for this year? Nothing big, are you? Like—a bicycle?"

He looked up, startled, as if he had not thought she was still there.

"Can't we wait, Mum?"

Can't we wait? What did he mean by that? Did any other child ever bring people up so short when they tried to talk to him?

" 'Can't we wait?' " she repeated, frowning. "I guess there'll be plenty of waiting. For anything as expensive as a bicycle."

"Can't we wait here 'til after Christmas?"

"Wait here? Oh, you mean stay here 'til after Christmas? Goodness, no. We'll be lucky if we get our stuff out before this lane is blocked full of snow. I don't like the looks of that sky a bit, right now." She glanced anxiously out of the window. "Moving is a terrible job, and when anybody's got it to do, the sooner it's done, the better. Think what fun it'll be getting up Christmas morning in a brand-new house. It won't be chilly upstairs there like it is here."

She smiled and shivered as she opened the stairway door.

Her voice and the tap of her quick steps echoed in the narrow passage.

"Hurry up," she was saying. "Eat your cereal before the bus comes. It's almost time for it to go over the lane."

Johnny sat as he was until there was no sound in the room.

Then he reached with a jerky motion for the milk pitcher. It was full and heavy and, as he poured, some of the milk spilled over onto the cracked oilcloth which covered the table. He watched a narrow white river flow out of the pool. As the river slowly broadened, brooks ran from it like twigs from the branches of a tree. One brook trickled close to the edge of the table. He took his handkerchief from his pocket and carefully, yet reluctantly, mopped up what had been spilled. He spread his left hand and looked at it, before he dropped the handkerchief over it as on a drying rack.

He was holding it there, looking at it, when his mother called, "Are you through, Johnny? The bus is going over!"

With his free right hand he dipped deep into the sugar bowl and sprinkled the gray island before him until it was as white as the waters which surrounded it.

There. It was all white. Perfectly white. Like the Arctic. Like the pearly gates. Like the coffin in which he had seen his infant brother lying. Like any far cold place where no one has ever been and returned.

He pushed back his chair and stood up, stuffing the handkerchief into his pocket.

He looked at the walls. The smudged last sheet of the calendar hung loosely on worn-out clips which once had pinioned a clean, full year. The rack, usually bulging with old newspapers, hung empty now that the best dishes had been wrapped and put in the barrel which stood in the sinkroom. The lounge his grandfather had made in his youth and lain on during the last weeks of his life was bare of cover and cushions. The braided mat was gone from before the stove. The knots in the pine floor looked up at Johnny like eyes with wrinkled lids; and the worn places where his mother's feet had pressed, and his grandmother's before her, were like hollows below cheek bones in a brown old face.

"Johnny!" his mother called. "The bus is coming up the hill. Did you eat all your cereal?"

He raised his head and turned it sharply from left to right.

He ran to the stairway door and pulled it open.

"Mum!" he called loudly.

"What? Your lunch is—"

"Mum—could I stay home today?"

His voice trembled.

She came to the head of the stairs and stood there, her hands on her hips.

"Johnny Lee," she said, "you may not stay home. You are not sick. You are never to play that game again. You know as well as I do what the principal said two months ago. He said it's the law that you have to go to school, and that feeling you get mornings is just trying to get out of going to school, and nothing else in this world. The doctor said so too. You don't have that feeling Saturday mornings. Now do you?"

Johnny shook his head, but the paleness of

his face and the size of his eyes frightened his mother. She sighed and let her hands fall.

"Oh, dear," she said. "Don't you feel good, honest?"

"Sure," Johnny said. He tried to smile at her. "I feel pretty good. I just thought—you got so much to do—can't I stay and—and help? I could take care of Deedy, couldn't I?"

The bus horn blew. The principal had given instructions to the bus driver as well as to Marge.

Johnny and his mother both jumped at the sound.

"No," his mother said with renewed determination. "Not on your tintype, young man. You do your job at school and I'll do mine here. When you get home I'll have a load ready for you and your father to take into town on the truck. Now grab your lunch and scoot!"

The horn blew again.

"Well,— 'bye," Johnny said.

"Quick!" his mother urged him.

She saw him close the door, heard him open others which he did not close, heard his running feet.

Then, from the yard: "Mum! Mum!"

"What is it, Johnny?"

" 'Bye, Mum!"

· 8 ·

"Good-bye, sonny! Hurry!"

"Yup . . . 'Bye, Mum—" faintly.

"Good-bye, Johnny!" she shouted.

Then she sank down on the top step, warming her arms against her breast. She was afraid again. She felt empty.

"Good-bye, darling," she whispered. "Good-bye, my baby. My precious, are you all right? What makes you look at me the way you do? Why can't you tell me what's the matter? I don't want to make you do anything you don't want to. I want you with me every minute just like Deedy is, and like you used to be. But that isn't right. Your father says if I don't look out you'll grow up a sissy; and the principal says you're smart and the reason you've got low marks is I've let you stay out of school so much. He says you might be on the honor roll if you went everyday. I used to be on the honor roll sometimes. I loved going to school. You'd like it if you got on the honor roll, wouldn't you, Johnny? I guess you'd be pretty proud of a card full of E's. I guess we would too. You're never going to be big and strong to do hard work like Daddy. He won't give in to that yet, but I have, Johnny. You're going to do a different kind of work. Maybe if you get good marks in school we'll manage to send you to college, and you'll

learn to be an expert accountant, or sell insur-
ance, or be a teacher—even a principal, like
Mr. Sturtevant. Think of that, Johnny! Some
day you'll be glad we made you go to school.
Some day we'll all be glad . . ."

She felt better. She thought of all she had to
do and ran downstairs.

The sight of Johnny's untouched cereal
moved her to healthy irritation.

"Johnny Lee!" she said aloud, sternly. "I
could shake you! I know what this means,—
you'll eat your lunch at recess and won't have
anything at noontime and come home hungry
as a bear, wanting cake or bread with apple-
sauce and brown sugar. Well, there won't be
any cake in this house tonight, nor any apple-
sauce; and the brown sugar is packed already.
So if you eat this afternoon, you'll eat just exactly what you left this morning!"

She set the white island in the white sea into
the cellar cupboard.

She was a sensible woman and she loved her
son very much. Too much to spoil him.

The baby woke and called, and Johnny's
mother ran upstairs again, snatched up the
warm, chubby creature, covered with kisses the
damp curls, pink cheeks, soft neck, and lively
fingers, and carried Deirdre to the warm kitch-

en on her shoulders, both of them laughing.

"Now, pet," Marge said, "we'll have our breakfast. You'll eat a nice big one, I know. You always do. And then you'll help me all day long. You and I've got heaps and piles to do, sweetie-pie. I'm going to bring in lots of boxes from the shed, and we'll fill them up. Because we're going tonight to live in a new house. A beautiful brand-new house. When we look out of the windows there, we won't see just old fields and trees. We'll see cars coming and going, and people walking by. You can wave to them and they'll wave back to you. It'll be just like it was where I lived when I was a little girl. Wave to Mummie, Deir."

Deirdre waved her spoon, ducking her head and looking merrily through her eyelashes.

"That's it," Marge cried in delight. "Oh, you darling. You adorable. You know what you are? You're what they write all the songs about. What would Mummie ever do without you?"

Marge went singing across the kitchen, her round face gentle, her blue eyes bright with love and eagerness, her step young and light, her voice clear and sweet. The room was no longer bare. It was not even the same room where Johnny had sat and stared around him. It was the room where he had once been as

Deirdre was now, but so long ago that the memory was like one of the dreams he had over and over, most of them bad but this one breathtakingly good. Bad or good, they were a part only of the nights. This was the room from which time had ejected him.

Johnny had gone to school.

His father came home about one o'clock, having asked for the afternoon off from the shipyard for the moving. Marge had cleared out the cupboards and warmed up the leftovers. Deirdre was having her nap. Marge met her big husband at the door with a hug, stood by the sink while he washed, telling him what she had done, and sat opposite him at the crowded table, her feet curled over the chair rung.

"As soon as these dishes are dry, I'll pack them," she said. "They're the last. All the bedding is into boxes, except Deir's. The clothes are in the trunks in the parlor. You can load this stuff any time and then I'll help you take the beds apart. They ought to be loaded last, so they'll come off first, and I can make them up while you come back for another load. I had a pie left, and I've just made a batch of biscuits, so with cheese and some bananas we can have a quick supper whenever you want to stop for it.

I must remember to keep the milk and coffee and coffee pot where I can put my hand on them. If we're sure of a bite to eat and beds to sleep in, we'll be all right until tomorrow. Then I can start fixing up . . . I don't know how you're going to get our big bedstead and mattress downstairs alone, Jack. I don't suppose it's ever been taken out since it was put up there."

"Whatever goes up must come down, they say," Jack grinned, over his coffee cup. "All you've done, I guess I can handle my end of it."

Jack did not often smile. He was a sober man, of few words. Marge knew he was proud of her and what she had done since morning. He was eating hugely. The flavor of good food, she thought, is even better the second day. She looked back at her husband radiantly and took another helping for herself. It was good to work hard and eat well, with a man like Jack. It would be fine when he did not have a farm to take care of, beside his job on the yard. They would keep just as busy. They liked to be busy. But they would go out together sometimes, to church and to meetings at Johnny's school and to the playground where there were sandboxes for Deir to dig in. She thought of how Jack would look, walking down the street beside her. He was very handsome. Town wives of pasty-faced store clerks and lily-handed bank cashiers would envy her. Her admiration shone in her eyes and colored her voice.

"Lucky for me," she said, "I married a guy with muscle. But don't you dare hurt your back or anything."

She began picking up the dishes.

"Oh, Jack, you don't know how I'm going to enjoy my stainless steel sink!"

As he went out to the truck with the first of the boxes, she was singing again.

But as the afternoon wore on, the strain of the long day began to be felt. They had both been up since daybreak. It started to snow and the truck skidded against the pump as Jack tried to turn it. He was some time getting it free, and a fender was bent until it cracked. Marge ran out to push and got her feet wet and had nothing dry into which to change unless she opened a trunk. A stock-dealer came for the two cows and the hens, and though he paid the price he had offered, he grumbled about it, saying the hens were moulting and one of the cows did not look to him as if she would give as much milk as Jack claimed.

"You can take my word about the cow or

you can get off my place," Jack said between his teeth.

He stood with his legs apart and his weight on his heels. His hands were thrust into his two back pockets as if he kept them there with difficulty. His plaid wool shirt flapped boldly in the icy wind.

Marge, in her wet shoes, shivered with cold and terror.

"As for the hens, what you expectin' to buy this time of year,—six weeks old chickens? These hens have laid good and they'll lay again. You goin' to sell hens to people that want eggs, or feather pillers? You come here last Tuesday night and we made a deal. These are the same hens and the same cows. Take 'em or leave 'em. But you hold your tongue; see?"

The fat little dealer pawed at the snow.

"Come now, Jack," he mumbled. "I didn't mean nuthin'. Only—"

"I've got no time for talk that don't mean nuthin'. You takin' this stock or bringin' it back to the barn?"

"Oh, I'm takin' it, Jack. Sure, I'm takin' it."

The dealer climbed hastily into his truck. As he turned out into the lane, he waved his hand.

"Good luck to ye in town, boy. If you ever want to come back to the farm and stock it again, let me know."

"He'll burn before I do," Jack muttered.

"Dear God, I thought you was going to fight," Marge said, in awe. "If you had, you'd have killed him."

"If he hadn't took it back, I would have," Jack said, throwing boxes and barrels into his truck. "Nobody's goin' to tell me—"

"Look out!" Marge cried. "That's the best dishes!"

Jack stopped. He stood over her.

"Get into the house," he told her. "Out of this snow. Haven't you got anything to do to keep out of my way? You want to get down sick in the middle of moving? You want to drive me crazy?"

"Jack Lee—"

"You heard me, Marge."

She ran away from him, stumbling. In the kitchen she cried a little.

"Why does he have to take it out on me," she whimpered, "what the dealer said?"

But then Deirdre woke up again and the sound of her small untroubled voice, the smoothness of her cheek, the very warmth of her blankets were a comfort to her mother.

"Well, honey lamb! . . . Well, honey lamb, you all ready to come to town to live? Go ride? Go bye-bye?"

In the yard Jack's fury was passing. The cows were gone. He had raised them from calves and milked them morning after morning, night after night, his forehead against their flanks. They would never have as good a home again as they had had with him. And he might never milk a cow again as long as he lived. If it had not been for Marge this would never have happened, either to him or to the cows. But he had made them cringe, the dealer and Marge too. Now the dealer had the cows and Marge had her way. Maybe it was a good way. Two jobs were too much for any man. Life would be easier with no barn to tend and no wood and water to carry. Johnny had never seemed to be much help on the farm. He wasn't stout and he wasn't handy. Marge thought it would be better for him, living in town; she thought he needed boys of his own age. Maybe he did; his father did not know what it was Johnny needed. Anyway, it would be nice for Marge, living where she had neighbors. No wonder she talked too much when he was around; the rest of the time, out here, she had nobody to talk to; she had never grown used to being alone. Probably it had been too much to ask.

He sighed.

He thought, "I'm gosh-darned tired. I wish the kid would get home. He ought to be able to take one corner of the mattress if his mother held one and I went ahead to carry the weight of it."

He went into the house, and when he saw that Marge had been crying, he touched her hair. It was pretty hair. The color of maple syrup.

"Did you change your shoes?" he asked her.

She shook her head, close to tears again.

"You go change 'em," he said gently. "Only take a minute. I'll watch Deedy. Then we'll take the beds apart. The rest of the first load is on."

It was as near to an apology as he ever made. It was near enough for Marge. She rubbed her chin against his arm as she passed him.

Before they had the beds apart, the school bus came but it went by the Lee place without stopping.

"For goodness' sake," Marge exclaimed in dismay. "Where on earth is Johnny? Jack, you don't suppose Miss Besse would keep him after school so he'd have to walk home in the storm? Johnny says she's threatened to, but I never thought she would."

"I'll find out," Jack said grimly. "If she did, I'll have a piece of her hide."

He rammed Johnny's folding bed into the space he had saved for it on the truck and stood by the lane as the bus came back. He held up his hand and the bus stopped.

"What you done with my boy?" he asked. "I need him."

Johnny would have liked to hear that.

"Why, he got off down the road apiece," the driver said. "With the Morris girl. Guess that's a love match, Jack. Guess you Lees start young."

He winked over his shoulder and several girls tittered. As the bus coughed and the driver shifted gears, a boy with dirty teeth leered at Jack, through the window, and made an obscene gesture.

Jack thought, "That Young Bill Sudbury. If I was Bill, I'd thrash him within an inch of his life."

But Jack was not Bill, and the bus was bearing Young Bill safely beyond Jack's reach.

Jack tramped back through the drifts and told Marge:

"The kid got off at Morris's road. Didn't you tell him there'd be work to do here to-night?"

She brushed her hair out of her eyes.

"I thought I did. I'm almost sure I did. He must know we're moving today!"

"I don't know what he knows," Jack growled. "His head's always in the clouds. Some time he's going to bump into something and bump hard . . . Well, maybe he'll be here when I'm ready for the mattress."

He wasn't, and Jack would not wait. He started down the stairs with the mattress on his back and lost his grip on it as he tried to go through the door. Marge ran, got her knee under one end, and somehow held it up off the snow until Jack could drag it onto the roof of the truck. She had not stopped for overshoes, and now her feet were wet again.

"What did you do that for?" Jack demanded when it was done. "Nobody asked you to. I could have carried it if you'd left me alone."

He could not tell her to change her shoes for she had no dry ones to change into. He could not tell her to dry her feet in the oven for they had let the fire go out, not daring to leave it burning when they closed the house.

They looked at each other in despair.

Then Johnny came into the yard. They heard his shuffling step, and turned their attention from each other to him.

They did not know how he had spent his day, except that he had been at school, that he had not been here while the work was being done, when the dealer had insulted his father and hauled Old Moll and Sparked away like so many cans of milk or so many pounds of beef, when his mother wept from hurt and fear and wet her feet doing what he might have done if he had been there and could give a hand where needed like most boys of his age. They only knew that he was coming back, late, now the work was done, shuffling slowly through the new snow.

He did not know how they had spent their day, except that they had had it—they and Deedy—here at home where a woodfire crackled and a teakettle sang; that the whole last day was gone and he had lost it.

He was coming into the yard as he had so many other nights, but it was no longer his yard. It was filled with a load of furniture which did not look familiar. It did not look alive. The yard belonged now to someone else. The house belonged to someone else. The barn belonged to someone else. And the pump, the apple trees, the stone walls, even the snow and the sky. He was a stranger here and belonged nowhere. All he had to belong to, to lean against, were his mother and his father.

He said, "Hi . . ."

"Where in tunket have you been?" his father demanded. "The last hour?"

"I—was in the woods. By Morris's—"

"With that Morris kid? All this time? What for? It's a good thing you're going to get away from her. You've hung onto her skirt ever since you could walk. Don't you know it's got everybody laughing at you? Why don't you try holding your own with some boys for a change? How you've ever rode two years on that bus with Bill Sudbury and never come home with a black eye or a bloody nose I'll never figure out. What do you do when he's around, anyway? Crawl?"

Johnny stood blinking.

His mother was sorry for him. She knew he could not fight Bill Sudbury. But why didn't he do what he could do?

"You said this morning you wanted to help," she reminded him reproachfully. "It doesn't look like it. Your father and I've done every single thing alone. After he'd worked half the day, too; and driven twenty miles. I don't know what you were thinking of, Johnny, not to get here as soon as you could. Seems as if even Deir's helped more than you have." She sighed. "Well, we're all ready. I'll go get my coat and bundle up Deir, and we may get there before dark."

She went wearily toward the house.

Johnny looked at his father.

"We—we going to stay down there when we go?"

"Stay? What do you think we're going for? The ride?"

"You—have you fed old Moll and Sparked?"

"Old Moll and Sparked are gone."

"Gone!"

Where had they gone?

"A lot you care," his father said. "You never even learned to milk 'em!"

He gave a sharp pull at the rope, trying to stretch it far enough to make a knot which would hold the mattress in place over the rough road.

"If I only had a few inches more," he grunted.

"Maybe," Johnny said in a stifled voice, "maybe I could find another piece—you could tie on—"

But Jack made what he had do, as he had learned he often could. He went into the house for his gloves, beating his bare hands against his sides. Marge was trying to pick up her handbag and the box which held their supper, while she held the baby on her arm.

"Daddy take," Deirdre said, holding out her hands. "Bye-bye now. Bye-bye now. Daddy take."

Jack laughed and took her. She gurgled.

"You know where you're well off, don't you?" he said.

"Now have we forgot," Marge asked, "anything we'll need tonight?"

"Don't worry," Jack told her. "I can come back if I have to. So far so good. Let's go."

"There's the lamps," Marge said. "You can get them tomorrow. We won't need them. Maybe we can sell them. Some people—oh, Jack, am I really going to have electricity at last?"

"You bet you are. Within an hour. Come on."

"I haven't left anything mice can get into —oh, there's a bowl of cereal I thought Johnny might eat. Well, I'll dump it out for the birds and take the bowl along. If he's hungry, I'll give him a biscuit out of the box . . .

I've got your teddy, Deir. All right; I'm coming."

She turned the key in the lock and dropped it into her handbag.

She climbed to the seat of the truck and Jack handed up the baby to her. He came around and slid in behind the wheel and started the engine.

Marge thought, "Now this is kind of cosy, all of us and our supper and our beds going to ride together. Those poor women who used to start off in covered wagons, worrying about Indians and not knowing when they would ever sleep in a house again! They weren't like us, with a new house waiting for us, a cement walk leading up to it, and electric lights and an electric stove and a bathroom in it. Goodness, I feel rested already just thinking about that house, in spite of all I've got ahead of me yet before I lay down!"

"Where've they got you tucked away, Johnny boy?" she asked cheerfully, peering into the back.

"Johnny!" his father exclaimed. "He went looking for a piece of rope as much as fifteen minutes ago. What is he, growing hemp to make it?"

He shouted, "Johnny! . . . JOHNNY!"

There was no answer.

Jack sprang down and strode back to the barn. The low rumble of the big door opening was a hollow sound.

"Johnny! You in here?"

From the dusky, dusty silence Johnny's eyes looked out. He was sitting on a barnacled, three-legged stool. Behind him was the mow of hay which had been sold with the farm. Beside him were the empty stanchions.

"What on earth are you doing, Johnny?"

Did he really miss those cows?

"I stopped . . . I just stopped to think . . ."

"What about?"

Jack rested his hand on his son's shoulder.

"About . . . oh, Dad, I never had my pony!"

Johnny began to cry. It was not that he wanted a pony now. He cried because he was too big even to want the pony which had once been promised him and which in imagination he had fed and watered in this barn so many nights and mornings and ridden so madly over fields and pastures and led so carefully when Linda sat astride the shaggy brown back; but which in actuality had never been his and now would never be. He cried for all the other joys and comforts he had longed for and which he was now too big ever to have, and yet too small for joys and comforts which come to those of size and power and experience and wisdom. He cried because he had been desolate, and because of his father's hand on his shoulder.

Jack looked down at him with mingled sympathy and exasperation.

He, too, had once wanted a pony, and he had never had one. But he had not really expected to have. He had known better. A child of six should know that a pony cost money and was of little use and that after a few years a boy's feet would drag on the ground if he tried to ride a pony. What kind of a nine-year-old was Johnny that he would huddle in a corner, on a day when so much was going on, and cry because he had not had a pony?

Jack took his hand away.

He said, "So you never had your pony. You've never had a kangaroo either, nor a king's crown, nor a yacht, nor a lump of gold. Neither have I and never expect to. Now put your boots out to that truck and stop snivelling. You've kept us waiting a quarter of an hour. It'll be dark before ever we get to the village, and then there'll be all the unloading and settling to do."

The door rumbled shut behind them. It had no lock, and never had had. Never until now had there been a night when a Lee would not have been roused from sleep by the movement of that door. But tonight nothing inside the barn was alive or of value. What little was there did not belong to Lees.

As Jack climbed into the truck and started the engine, Marge whispered, "Where'd you find him? He's been crying, hasn't he?"

"Yeah," Jack muttered. "Sitting there crying because he never had a pony. What's ever going to become of him beats me."

"I guess he just said that. It just happened to come into his head. He probably feels bad, in some ways, to leave the farm. Like all of us."

Jack watched the ruts. He knew that he was the only one who felt bad about leaving the farm. Marge had never liked it. Deirdre was too young to know one place from another. Johnny had never tried to milk the cows, though Old Moll had been gentle as a kitten and gave down almost at a touch as if she was glad to. He drove faster.

"All comfy, Johnny?" Marge called back. "You must be hungry. Here's a biscuit. You be thinking what you want for Christmas. Of course nothing that would cost too much. Like a bicycle."

Johnny took the biscuit. He bit into it and chewed. It clung to his tongue and teeth, a gluey mass. He could not swallow it. Finally he took it out, made it into a dozen little balls, and dropped them, one at a time, through the crack in the truck floor. The rest of the biscuit he squeezed between his hands, then picked it apart, and dropped the crumbs through the crack. He thought of Hansel. And he thought of Linda, who was Gretel. Only Gretel had not come with Hansel. If she had, he would be happy even if they starved, even if they froze to death in the wilderness. Because whatever happened to them would happen to them both. Gretel would go with him, if necessary, even into a witch's oven, her hand cool on his, her eyes full of courage and compassion. Gretel loved whatever Hansel loved, and what he feared she hated. Hansel was incapable of hate. That was why the witch would get him. Because he was alone.

It grew pitch dark inside the truck. He rested his head on his knees.

The kitchen was gone. The farm was gone. The lane was gone. Even the little grotto he and Linda had found in the woods near her house that day—the tiny, grassy room under a roof of ice where Linda said a winter fairy lived. They had cut their hands tucking in a fairy's carpet of moss, a fairy's bed of pine needles, a fairy's table of birch bark, a fairy's acorn cups and saucers; that too, was gone.

Johnny tried to get the grotto back.

Pressing his eyes against his knees he saw pinpricks of light begin to whirl, growing larger with every revolution, until they were wheels flashing faster and faster and merging into one big wheel of incredible brilliance. Within the wheel as within a priceless frame gleamed the white ice of the grotto roof, and through it he could see the winter fairy setting her birchbark table for supper, filling two acorn cups, turning back the blankets on her pine needle bed. She moved gracefully across the velvet floor. Gracefully and slowly. She was waiting for someone to come. She tipped her tiny head to listen for his knock . . . He knocked. She spread her iridescent wings and flew to the door. She cried, "Oh, darling, come in! I'm so glad you're here!" She reached up and put her arms around his neck. But she had to reach up only a very little, because he was hardly taller than herself. He closed the door and a bell tinkled with the closing. The sound was sweeter than any music, even bird songs. And so was Linda's voice. She said, "There. They can't get us now, Johnny. Nobody can ever find us now. . . ."

"Johnny!" his mother called. "I declare, Jack, he's asleep, for all that bumping and lurching! Wake up, Johnny! Here's our new house!"

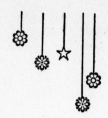

Saturday

2

$\mathcal{T}$HE next forenoon everyone was very busy. Jack drove back to the farm for the front room furniture and Johnny wanted to go with him but his father said the man next door had offered to help; it would take two men to handle the upholstered sofa and the big cherry table and Margie's parlor organ.

So Johnny stayed in the new house and followed his mother about. He spread out the rugs but they were not placed as she wanted them and had to be changed. She let him help unwrap the dishes and hand them to her to put away in the cupboards, and she worried for fear he would break them. He did drop one—one of the set—but it did not break. She said a piece of the border got chipped, but he thought the chip had been there when he took off the paper.

He wanted to talk about all that had happened to these dishes, where they had been before, the trip they had taken, but his mother was too busy to listen. So he pretended the dishes could feel and think and hear, and talked to them.

"It's all right, Mrs. Cup," he said. "Mr. Saucer is on the way up. Don't you worry, Mrs. Cup. Mr. Saucer, you go take care of Mrs. Cup. You tell her that shelf isn't a dark place. It just looks like a dark place. She got kind of scared staying in the barrel. You tell her everything's all right . . . Come on, Red Sugar Bowl. You're not scared, Red Sugar Bowl. You're brave . . . Hi, Deedy's Mug! Deedy wondered last night where you'd gone to, Mug! Did you think you didn't have Deedy any more? Well, you do. She's right over there in her playpen. See? I'll take you to Deedy—"

"Don't, Johnny," his mother said. "She'll only get it dirty. Give it to me."

"That's Deedy's Mum, Mug. You go to Deedy's Mum. Deedy'll have you when she eats her dinner. You'll be with Deedy then, just like you used to be. You won't be lonesome any more, Mug. You'll be with Deedy."

"Johnny!" his mother exclaimed at last. "That's silly. You're getting me so muddled up I don't know what I'm doing. Here it is 'most noontime. Your father'll be back any minute and I haven't got a thing together to eat."

He was quiet after that.

He went into the dining-room. It seemed strange to be in a house which had a dining-room. There had been none at the farm; just the big kitchen and sinkroom, the sitting-room where people sat only in warm weather, the front room where people went on great occasions, the back bedroom where his grandfather had slept, and two chambers upstairs. Because there had been no dining-room at the farm, this one was empty. His mother hoped to buy furniture for it by and by. A big table, she said, with six chairs and a sideboard. He had asked what a sideboard was for and she said to keep silver and tablecloths and napkins in, and to put flowers and candles on. He wondered where the flowers would come from. He wondered if the candles would be lit at night.

He went on into the living-room. This, too, was empty, but today the front-room furniture would come and fill it up. He did not feel at all well acquainted with the front-room furniture. At the farm his mother had kept it covered with old sheets. Sometimes he had opened the door to look in. The sight had fascinated even as it terrified him. Ghostly chairs, shrouded couch, a table in which he could see his eyes and teeth, ivory keys yellowed by time, ebony keys gray with age. He shivered. In a living-room would sheets be spread?

He would rather have the sitting-room furniture here. This was a warm room, a brighter one than the front-room at the farm. It had a new, clean, square little fireplace. With the sitting-room furniture it would look all year as the sitting-room had in summer. The willow rocker with the green plush seat; the wicker rocker resting in its stand; the phonograph with the big horn and the black and brown cylinder records which his grandfather had loved to hear him play; the Larkin desk with all the pigeon holes and the shelves below where he had kept his toys and books and striped bags of candy behind a flowered curtain . . . But his mother had said the sitting-room furniture was not worth moving; that she would be ashamed for village people to see it; that there was no place to store it in the new house.

The living-room had three windows side by side. They filled one whole end. He turned his back on the room and stood looking out at the sidewalk and the street. Cars were coming and going. People he did not know went by without turning their faces. A boy he had seen at school—an older boy—sat on the railing of the porch across the way. He wore a cap with a visor and earlappers. He stared at the house where Johnny was and suddenly caught sight of Johnny. He looked surprised. He gave a shout and another boy came running from a vacant lot. They scooped up snow and made two hard balls which they threw with deadly aim. The balls came splat! splat! against the window before Johnny's face. The snow was wet, and stuck there.

He blinked, but did not move. He stood, impaled on his own fear, between the snow-covered glass and the ghosts of the front-room furniture haunting the emptiness behind him.

Then his mother called, "Johnny! Dinner's ready! Your father hasn't come yet, but we might as well eat."

He wheeled blindly, and ran.

She was by the stove in the kitchen.

It was a small white stove, not a big black stove. No fire crackled in it. But she was there. The same teakettle sang. There was the same smell of crisping bacon, of toasting bread, of

· *39* ·

cheese and apples. Deirdre was pounding on her highchair tray with her spoon as she always did at meal time.

Johnny's breath came more evenly.

He slid into his chair at the table and felt the warmth of his mother's body as she reached across his shoulder to put a glass of milk beside his plate. His own pink glass. He liked pink glass. It made the milk look rosy.

He smiled up at his mother.

"Gee, Mum," he said. "I bet you're tired."

"Don't mention it," she said. "There's still so much to do I don't know which way to turn."

She pulled Deirdre's chair up beside hers and gave Deirdre a piece of toast, a strip of bacon.

She sat with her right arm resting on the back of Deirdre's chair, and lifted her tea cup wearily with her left hand.

Johnny thought her arm looked very soft. He would have liked to lean his head against it, to rub his cheek against it. He wondered that Deirdre chewed her bacon absorbedly, unaware of her mother's nearness.

"I don't know what's taking your father so long," Marge said.

"I guess," Johnny ventured, "he'll be here any time now."

"Yes, and then we'll have to start on the living-room. I hope we can get the pictures hung. I want to get the curtains up. Somebody might call tomorrow. People do that in town when new folks move in. I wish I had new curtains. But the old ones looked fairly good after I did them up. I mended two or three places. Just small ones. They probably won't show. I'm afraid they're a mite short for those windows, though . . ."

He loved to hear her voice. He loved the way it ran on and on, as if she were thinking aloud. Sometimes he suspected that his father tired of it, but he never did. It flowed smoothly, like a small, quiet river. If only he could always hear it! If only . . . If only it would come closer! . . . If only he could feel it laving his feet, his back, his chest, his shoulders as it had when she gave him his baths! It had not seemed to him then that she bathed him with water from the tank at the end of the stove, but with her soft voice and with something crystal clean and heavenly sweet-smelling which flowed from herself . . .

Suddenly—it seemed sudden to Johnny because he had not been following her words but her tone—she said:

"Isn't it time for your report card?"

He looked at his plate, surprised to find it empty of all she had put on it, and nodded slowly.

"I thought you always got it a week before vacation."

He did. And he had got it yesterday. He and Linda had stood together in the woods, looking at the two yellow cards marked off in little squares. Linda had two E's and all the rest G's. E's and G's were beautiful letters, the way Miss Besse made them. He was proud of Linda's beautiful card. He had put his arm around her and said, "Gee, Linda, you're smart."

Linda had looked at the letters on his card and shaken her head.

"You're smarter'n I am," she had said. "Miss Besse's mean. Never mind, Johnny. Next year we'll have Mrs. Curtis. Everybody says she's nice. If only she don't resign. I guess she's getting pretty old . . ."

"Johnny!" his mother exclaimed. "You haven't lost that card, have you?"

He wished he had. He wished it had been dropped into the grotto. There the winter fairy would have brushed it with magic and turned all the letters into E's. It would have become so beautiful that she would have laughed aloud, and they would have hung it on their shining wall to look at and to admire forever.

"Johnny?"

"No'm. It's—I guess it's in my jacket pocket."

"Well, go get it this minute. It makes a terrible lot of work for the teacher if a card is lost, and with the way everything has been turned upside down—"

Johnny looked about the strange room. In the kitchen at home his jacket had always hung on a hook behind the stove.

"I don't know where my jacket is."

"Oh, for goodness' sake! It ought to be in the coat closet!"

But it wasn't. They hunted a long time for the jacket. It seemed to Marge that Johnny looked for it only in the middle of the floor. Finally she pulled it out from a pile of patchwork quilts.

"There. Here it is. Damp, too. I suppose it's dampened the bedding. I'll have to air the quilts now, before I put them away . . . Oh, dear, Johnny, here are two dirty handkerchiefs. Awfully dirty handkerchiefs. One of them smells sour. What in the world . . .

And here's your card, all curled up. I declare,
Johnny Lee, you don't seem to—"

He saw the pupils of her eyes focussing on
the small squares. Reading . . . Spelling . . .
Music . . . History . . . Arithmetic . . .Effort
. . . School Citizenship . . . Days Absent . . .
Days Tardy . . .

At least, for the first time, he had not been
absent.

He said, "I didn't miss a day. Did I, Mum?
And I wasn't ever late!"

"You can't be late if you catch the bus," she
said irritably. "And the bus waits for you!"

She sighed.

"No, and you didn't miss. I saw to that. Mr.
Sturtevant said if you didn't stay out your
marks would be better. They aren't a bit better. They're—why, they're just exactly the
same as last time. Not one single E . . . Only
one G, and that's in music . . . All the rest
F's, even in reading. In the summer your father says you always have your nose stuck in
a book, and in school you get F in reading! F
in effort, too . . . There, Johnny. There's the
answer right there. You don't try, at school.
Do you, Johnny? You don't try; do you?"

*Do you . . . You don't try, do you . . .
Do you . . . You don't try, do you . . .*

"Johnny?"

". . . I don't know."

"You don't know! You don't even know whether you try or not! Well, I can tell you I know I try, and I know your father tries. We've tried all our lives, at school and since we couldn't go to school any more. We're trying to give you chances we never had. We've sold the farm—and your father loved that place—so you could live in town and learn nice ways to act and ride a bicycle and go to movies and get an education. Sometimes I've thought you might go to college. Mr. Sturtevant says the tests showed you could! But if you keep on this way, you won't even pass in high school. If you won't even try—"

Tears of disappointment and helplessness came into her eyes. She whirled and turned a faucet. The water gushed out of it, icy cold. She splashed it over her face and groped for a towel. She turned another faucet and the water ran warm. It was almost as magical as anything a winter fairy could do. She wet a cloth and came back to the table to wipe Deirdre's face and hands. She bent and kissed the top of Deirdre's head.

"Mum," Johnny said hoarsely.

She did not answer.

"Mum . . . Could I go to the show?"

She glared around at him.

She said, "The show? No, you may NOT! I'm going to write out some words and give you a pencil and paper and set up the card table in the dining-room, and you're going to write nice and spell right before you're through or I'll know the reason why. Now hang your jacket in the closet where it belongs."

He took his jacket and hung it up, but it did not look as if it belonged there.

When he came back into the kitchen, his mother was writing at the table. The point of her pencil was sharp. He could hear it cutting into the yellow paper as she wrote. She wrote across the top of eight lined sheets.

"Now," she said, at last. "Take these, and copy every one times enough to fill the page. When you're through, I'll look at them. If they're not written nice, you can just do them over. Then I'll hear you spell the words."

He took the papers into the dining-room.

His mother's writing was very round and plain. It was almost as beautiful as Miss Besse's.

A boy must try to do well.

I go to school to study.

My teacher helps me all she can.

My mother wants me to try hard.

My father is very good to me.

Christmas is a week from Sunday.

I have a little sister.

We have come to live in town.

They were not long sentences. There were no hard words in them. He did not know why they made him want to cry.

After a while he lapped his pencil and began to write.

A boy must try to do well. A boy must try to do well. A boy must try to do well . . .

A truck stopped before the door. The engine raced. His father and another man began bringing in the front-room furniture. They stamped the snow off their feet. They talked and laughed and swore. They paid no attention to Johnny.

A boy must try to do well. A boy must try to do well.

They had been back to the farm. They could go back to the farm because they were big and strong. Johnny could not go back to the farm.

A boy must try to do well. A boy must try to do well.

The farm was sold. The house was sold. The

kitchen was gone. The grotto was buried deep under snow. The winter fairy was safe inside, but she was alone. Nobody came to her. Nobody knocked at her door. She sang a sad song, like Redwing.

A boy must try to do well. A boy must try to do well.

When all the furniture was unloaded, and his father had thanked the neighbor and the neighbor had gone home, his mother came through the room with Deirdre in her arms. She did not look at Johnny.

My mother wants me to try hard. My mother wants me to try hard. My mother wants me to try hard.

She stood between the empty dining-room and the crowded living-room, patting Deirdre's back and talking to his father.

"Well, that's a good forenoon's work. That's all of it, isn't it? Lucky we had good weather today. The sofa fits fine under the windows, doesn't it? I thought it would. Well, now, Jack, you must be starved. Come on out and eat. I just made fresh coffee. I'll have a cup with you, soon as Deir's tucked in bed."

My mother wants me to try hard. My mother wants me to try hard.

"I've accomplished a lot too. The dishes are

all out of the barrels and on the shelves. After you've eaten I'll clean up. It's just nothing to get a meal on an electric stove and wash up with running hot and cold water. Honestly, Jack, I didn't realize—and Deir had such fun in the bathtub this morning. I really think she was swimming. You ought to have seen her. You will tomorrow."

My mother wants me to try hard. My mother wants me to try hard.

She hurried back through the dining-room. His father followed her, pulling off his gloves.

"What you doing, Johnny?" his father asked. "Why don't you get outdoors, a nice winter day like this? Afraid somebody'll throw a snowball at you?"

Did he know?

"He's staying in," his mother called crisply from the kitchen, "because I told him to. He's going to learn to write, and he's going to learn to spell. He's got his report card, and it's all F's again. Except in music."

"Can't he learn to write and spell in five days a week," his father asked, "and learn something else on Saturdays?"

But he had gone on into the kitchen and was washing in the warm water which ran so richly from the faucet into the stainless steel sink.

My father is very good to me. My father is very good to me. My father is very good to me . . .

I go to school to study . . .

My teacher helps me all she can . . .

I have a little sister . . .

We have come to live in town . . .

Deirdre had her nap. His father finished his dinner and they talked and laughed over the coffee cups. They did the dishes together and Marge did not worry for fear Jack would break any of them. Or, if she did, she did not say so, for if she had, he would have stopped drying them. They talked about how good Mr. Schultz had been to help with the heavy moving and not to take a cent in pay. They thought the Schultzes would be fine neighbors. Marge hoped Mrs. Schultz would come to call as soon as the living-room curtains were hung. Mr. Schultz had told Jack he had a boy, Kenny, about Johnny's age. Jack said he was relieved that Johnny was where he could play with boys like Mr. Schultz's son. Too many country boys nowadays were like Bill Sudbury's. A different class lived in the country now than had when Jack was growing up.

Johnny was still writing.

They talked about how cheaply they had managed the moving and how they would earn and save the money to make up the difference between what the farm had brought and what they had paid for this house. Jack said he thought they would have the mortgage cleaned up in a year's time. He reminded Marge of the double garage they had here, and they planned the advertisement they would put in the village paper. Jack said they ought to get ten dollars a month from somebody who needed a place to keep his car.

Marge said, "Every little bit helps, doesn't it? Now let's see if we can get that living-room in shape. Oh, Jack, we might be all settled before dark!"

She squeezed his hand. Their two hands were still together when they came through the room where Johnny sat writing.

We have come to live in town. We have come to live in town.

"Of course, it's partly because we haven't much to settle. It'll be a long time before we can afford a dining-room set."

"I'll tell you what, Marge. You can have

what we get from renting the garage for your dining-room set."

"Jack! You mean it?"

Jack was feeling fine.

"Why not?"

"Don't you need it for the mortgage?"

"Hundred and twenty dollars would buy the set, wouldn't it? It wouldn't make much of a dent in the mortgage. Heck, no; I'll take care of the mortgage by another Christmas. You rent your garage and get your dining-room set."

"Jack, you darling!"

She hugged him.

Jack looked sheepishly over her head at his son.

" 'Most done, Johnny?"

Johnny shook his head.

"Can't you let him off, Marge? He ought to be outdoors. Come on. It's Saturday. Give him a break."

"We-ell," his mother said, turning her head, her cheek against his father's shoulder.

"I want to finish," Johnny said quickly, urgently. "I don't want to go out, Mum. I'm writing it nice. I'll finish pretty soon. Then you can hear me spell."

"Why, he's really trying, Jack," his mother

said proudly. "Leave him alone. He's a good boy."

She pulled his ear gently as she passed on her way to the living-room. She looked down at the spread papers.

My teacher helps me all she can. My teacher helps me all she can.

"It's nice writing," she said. "It's real nice writing. Look, Jack!"

"Hm. Good enough. Better than I could do. What does he need to be such a blamed good writer for?"

"So he'll get E in it on his next report card," his mother beamed. "So he'll be on the honor roll and go up to high school with his class."

"Then they'll teach him to use a typewriter, won't they?" his father asked. "And he'll never write more than his name again. What the sense of it is beats me. But if he wants to—"

His mother patted Johnny's shoulder.

"Funny boy," she said. "You've done a few lines on every sheet, and you haven't finished any of them. What kind of a way to do is that?"

"I will," he said. "I'm going to."

" 'Course you are."

She went on into the next room.

He wanted to write fast, so that she would come back to hear him spell. But he could not write fast, because he must write beautifully.

My mother wants me to try hard. My mother wants me to try hard.

We have come to live in town. We have come to live in town.

Johnny called, "Mum!"

They did not hear him. They were putting up picture hooks.

"Mum!"

"What is it?"

"I thought of something."

"What?"

"If you've got to wait a whole year for the dining-room set, why don't Daddy bring down the things from the sitting-room to put in here?"

"Oh . . . I don't want them, Johnny."

"Just until you get the set, I mean."

"Oh, no. We don't want that old stuff in a nice house like this. I'd rather go without 'til I can have what's right. I'll tell you what I thought, Jack. We can buy another card table. They don't cost much and they always come in handy. Then if we want company to a meal, I could serve it on the two card tables in front of the fireplace here. Lots of people do that way. I've read about it in the magazines. Even people that have dining-room furniture."

"Okay by me. As long as we eat, I don't care where we eat. What next?"

"Let's see how the curtains look. They're in that suitbox."

We have come to live in town. We have come to live in town. We have come to live in town.

Johnny kept on writing for a long time. He had still not finished when the doorbell rang.

"Goodness!" his mother exclaimed. "Callers already? You go to the door, Jack, while I run fix myself a little."

She fluttered through the room where Johnny sat.

His father opened the door and a deep, pleasant voice said, "How do you do? Is this Mr. Lee? I'm Howard Shawn. Pastor of the Methodist Church."

"Oh, yes. Well, come in, Reverend. Come in."

They went into the living-room.

"Just moved to town, have you, Mr. Lee?"

"Into the village, yes. I've always lived in

the town. And my folks before me. On a farm up back here. About four miles."

"That's what I heard. I'm new in town myself. This is my first pastorate, as a matter of fact. I only graduated from the seminary last June."

"That so? Thought you looked like a young feller."

"Shouldn't wonder if we're about the same age.

"No. No, I'll never see thirty again."

"Is that a fact? Why, I was just thinking you couldn't be the Jack Lee I'd heard about. Jack Lee who had a son in our primary department."

Johnny's mother went quietly through the room where Johnny sat writing. She had brushed her hair out. It glistened. She had put pink color on her mouth. She was smiling a little.

"This is my wife," Jack said.

"How do you do, Mrs. Lee. I'm Howard Shawn of the Methodist Church—"

"Oh, how do you do, Mr. Shawn! Didn't Jack take your hat? Here, let me. And your coat, too; or you won't feel it when you go out—"

"I'll only stop a minute. Moving day is a busy day."

"Oh, we're just enjoying it. You'll excuse our not being all settled, won't you? It's nice of you to call so promptly on newcomers."

"Well, I know how it is. I'm a newcomer too."

They all laughed. It sounded bright and cosy. Johnny could not see them, but he could hear them.

Christmas is a week from Sunday. Christmas is a week from Sunday. Christmas—

"Is your son at home?"

"Johnny? Yes. He's—studying."

"Studying on Saturday? That's unusual. I hoped he would be here. I wanted to meet him. He is on our Sunday School roll. I suppose he hasn't been able to get there since the churches gave up sending buses into outlying districts. But he's still our boy, and I hope that now he has come within easy walking distance of us, we'll see him often."

"Well, I hope so, I'm sure. I don't know. He hasn't spoken of it. I know he did go to the Methodist quite a while, and then he changed over to the Baptist, because that was where the little girl he played with went. Children are like that, I guess. But since they stopped sending the bus he hasn't been anywhere."

Jack said, "There's an awful lot to do on a

· 57 ·

farm Sundays, when a man works away the rest of the week."

"I don't doubt that. Now things ought to be a little easier. Maybe we'll see you all at church tomorrow."

"Well, not tomorrow, I guess. I have to stay with the baby, and Jack's got to haul some wood before he gets back to work Monday."

"I take it you're planning to light up this nice little fireplace. I love an open fire. It's a real inspiration . . . Could you get Johnny to leave his books and come in for a minute, I wonder?"

"Why, of course."

Johnny's mother came to the dining-room door. She smiled and held out her hand.

"The minister wants to see you, sonny," she said.

She waited until he reached her and drew him into the living-room with her arm across his shoulders. Johnny felt like a bird in a nest.

He blinked.

The late afternoon sunshine was streaming in. The front room furniture was not covered with sheets. He had always thought the upholstery of the sofa and the two big chairs was dark blue, but it was quite a bright blue, and velvety flowers like small daisies stood out all over

· 58 ·

them. The curtains were milk-white and stiffly starched. There was a white lace runner on the long table. A rug he had never seen lay before the fireplace. It had a dog on it. A curly brown dog with floppy ears.

The man sitting on one end of the sofa, with a soft black hat on his knees, was young and his hair was red.

"This is Johnny, Mr. Shawn," his mother said.

"Hello, Johnny. I've been wanting to meet you. I'm new at the Methodist church, and you used to come there to Sunday School, didn't you?"

Johnny cleared his throat.

"Sometimes," he said carefully.

Mr. Shawn was leaning toward him. He was smiling. There was nothing but friendliness in his face.

"Yes. That's what I heard. You came pretty regularly for a year or more, didn't you?"

"I guess so."

"Well, I just wanted you to know that we're glad you've come to town to live. If you want to go somewhere else to Sunday School, that's fine. I just hope you'll go somewhere to Sunday School tomorrow. It's a pretty nice place to be on Sunday morning, isn't it? Our Sunday

School begins at 11:00 when the grown-ups have their service upstairs. I think the Baptist Sunday School is at 12:00 after the morning service. Both places the children sit together and sing and then somebody plays the piano for our children to march off to their different class rooms. I imagine they do the same at the Baptist Church, don't they?"

"Yes, sir."

"You like to sing and march?"

"Yes, sir."

"Johnny loves music," said his mother proudly. "He gets G in music at school all the time."

"Well, that's pretty fine. I'll bet he has a good voice to sing, hasn't he? What do you say, Johnny, if we try to get your mother to play something you can sing?"

"Goodness," his mother said, pleased. "I haven't had any time to practise since Deir was born. I don't know how the old organ stood the trip, either. But I guess I can play any hymn that doesn't have more than two sharps or four flats. What do you want to sing for Mr. Shawn, Johnny?"

"I don't know. I can't sing very good."

His mother laughed.

"He's shy," she said.

"Most people are, about singing alone," said Mr. Shawn. "I am myself. But I love to sing."

He was over by the organ, looking through the hymn book. Johnny's mother was on the stool with her hands folded in her lap.

Johnny was by the door, alone.

Mr. Shawn looked over the edge of the book. His eyes were as blue as the upholstery.

"Johnny," he said, "do you suppose your father could stand it if you and I sung 'Faith of Our Fathers'? You know that, don't you? The tune anyway?"

Johnny nodded.

"Sure. Go ahead," Jack said. "I like singing. Always did."

"The words are kind of hard," said Mr. Shawn. "Any we can't pronounce we'll just skim over."

He was holding out his hand to Johnny as his mother had in the dining-room. When Johnny was beside him, he too put his arm around Johnny. It felt different from his mother's, but in some ways better. Now he was between the two of them.

" 'Faith of our fathers, living still
'In spite of dungeon, fire and sword,

'O how our hearts beat high with joy
'Whene'er we hear that glorious word . . .' "

The minister's voice rang out triumphantly.
Johnny's trembled. At the end of the first
chorus Mr. Shawn drew Johnny hard against
him for an instant, sharing his strength, his
triumph over dungeon, fire and sword . . .

In the second verse, Mr. Shawn sang more
softly, Johnny more steadily.

" ' . . . And through the truth that comes
from thee
'Mankind shall then indeed be free.' "

This time Mr. Shawn's pressure was gentler,
briefer, as if he sensed that Johnny now had
what he needed, and were set free.

The last verse Johnny sang alone, in a clear,
pure soprano.

" 'Faith of our fathers, we will love
'Both friend and foe in all our strife
'And preach thee, too, as love knows how
'By kindly word and virtuous deed . . .' "

Mr. Shawn came in with the bass on the
final chorus, accompanying Johnny, the two

of them not quite touching, each standing straight and at his full height, but still together.

As Marge took her hands reluctantly from the smooth old keys, Jack said, "Well, what was the matter with that?"

Mr. Shawn was looking down at Johnny in gentle amazement.

"This boy," he said, and stopped. "This boy has a fine voice. Fine feeling, too. And he read every one of those big words as well as I could. That's remarkable for a third-grader. You must be very proud of this youngster."

"Well," his mother said, "of course we are." But she was embarrassed. She stood up from the stool. "We've got a nice baby girl, too, Mr. Shawn. I hear her waking up now. You sit down and I'll bring her down to show you."

I have a little sister. I have a little sister.

"I'm afraid I have to go, Mrs. Lee," said Mr. Shawn, looking at his watch. "My wife is entertaining the other ministers and their wives at dinner tonight. She'll want me there a little early. I'll call again soon, and see the baby then. I like babies, but, to tell the truth, I'm more interested in boys. Especially boys like yours. Good-bye, Mrs. Lee. Good-bye, Mr. Lee. You've got a nice place here . . . Good-bye, Johnny. Thanks for singing with me. There's a lot in that hymn, isn't there? You'll be singing in some Sunday School tomorrow, won't you?"

"Sure," Johnny said. "In yours. I'll come to yours."

"You will? Well, it's up to you, son. But we'd be mighty glad to have you."

He went down the little path, putting on his hat. As he reached the sidewalk he turned and saw Johnny still standing in the doorway. He smiled and swung his hand.

"Good-bye, Johnny," he said again. "See you tomorrow."

"Shut the door, Johnny," his mother called. "Before I bring Deir downstairs. You're letting cold in."

He closed it slowly, and went back into the living-room. Surely it would not still look as it had when Mr. Shawn was in it.

But it did. The upholstery waved its velvety blue daisies. The curtains and the lace were milk-white. The hymn book lay open to "Faith of Our Fathers." The organ keys looked warm from his mother's hands. The ears of the dog on the rug seemed to twitch. Indeed, Mr. Shawn seemed to be there. At least, though the sun had gone down, there was still a radiance in the room.

Was that faith the faith of Johnny's father?

"Tell you what, son," his father said, "let's surprise the womenfolks. Let's have a fire here when they come downstairs. I brought a few birch sticks and some kindling on the load this morning. It's in a box in the bottom of the closet."

"Okay," Johnny cried. "Okay, Dad!"

He brought the box. He knelt beside the dog on the rug, careful not to pinch the floppy ear. He twisted paper as his father was doing to make a small flat heap in the center of the bricks, and placed the kindling crisscross of the paper, watched his father lay on a small, speckled log and scratch a match on the sole of his shoe.

The flame sprang up, spread softly through the paper, clung to the kindling, and crackled over the birch bark.

"Nothing like a wood fire," said his father, putting the box away.

"No," said Johnny, on his knees.

"You can't beat it," said his father, coming back and sitting down to light his pipe, "with oil, nor coal, nor anything else."

"No," said Johnny. "I don't think so either, Dad."

"It's got a good sound to it. Like it means business."

"Like popcorn," said Johnny. "Like when we were blocked in with snow up home. And you'd get the popper from the shed chamber. Did we bring our popper?"

"I don't know's we did. I'll have to look for it tomorrow when I go up for the wood."

"You'd better. That's a good popper. Can I go with you when you go up tomorrow?"

"Depends on when I go. If I have to go in the morning, you'll be in Sunday School, won't you? Or won't you?"

Jack's eyes twinkled. Johnny knew his father did not hold much with churches.

But Johnny said, "Yeah. I guess I will."

He wanted to go to the farm, but not as much as he had this morning. He wanted more to go to Sunday School. Mr. Shawn's Sunday School.

His mother came down with Deirdre, and they were both surprised to see the fire. Deirdre crowed and kept creeping toward it. Her mother sat down on the floor to see that she did not creep too close. It was nearly dark now, outside, but in the new living-room the fire crackled and sang and made all their faces rosy with its heat and light.

"Now this," said Jack, "is solid comfort."

"My supper's cooking while we sit here," said Marge contentedly. "And you don't have to think of going out to do chores . . . Mr. Shawn was real nice, wasn't he?"

"Pretty good joe," Jack said, "for a minister."

Johnny waited to see if they would say anything about the singing.

But just then Deirdre said, "Go home now. Go ride. Bye-bye, Daddy. Deedy bye-bye now."

She pulled herself up by her father's knee.

"No, ma'am," he said. "No bye-bye tonight. Daddy's got his slippers on."

She looked at his shoes, puzzled. She looked searchingly into his face.

"Go home," she said distinctly. "Go ride, Daddy. Go home. Deedy home."

"Ride on my knee," he said, and put her there, bouncing her up and down.

But she pulled away from him and slid to the floor. She began to cry and crept swiftly toward her mother.

"Mum-Mum! Deedy home! Deedy home!"

"I declare, Jack," her mother exclaimed, "do you suppose she honestly—where's teddy, Deir? Where's your teddy, sweetie-pie? Here's teddy!"

Deirdre pushed the teddy-bear away, and dragged at her mother's arm, crying.

"Ho-ome! Deedy home. Bye-bye now."

Her mother tried to cuddle her, but Deirdre kept on crying.

"Come over and look out our nice windows, honey. See the lights? See the pretty lights?"

"Dark," sobbed Deirdre. "All dark. Home now. Go home."

"Turn on the lights, Jack."

The lights in the room flashed on.

Johnny blinked.

"Dark now," sobbed Deirdre. "Go home. Go home. Deedy home."

"Well!" her mother said. "I don't know what to do with her. She'll just have to get over it. I've got supper to take up. You two see she keeps away from the fire."

Jack put a chair on its side across the front of the hearth.

"You watch her, Johnny," he said.

He followed Marge into the kitchen, closing the door behind him. He liked to see her taking up a meal.

Crying, Deirdre crept to the door and pounded on it.

"Daddy! . . . Mum-Mum! Deedy—go—home—now!"

"Why, Deedy!" Johnny said.

She looked at him in surprise. He knew how she felt. She had thought she was alone.

"You said a whole sentence," he told her. "A whole great big sentence. All yourself."

She stopped crying, but her underlip was still thrust out.

She said doubtfully, "All dark, D'onny! Go home!"

He nodded, holding out his hand to her as Mr. Shawn had to him.

"Sure it's dark," he said. " 'Most supper time. Mum's getting supper. 'Most time for Deedy to go to sleep. Deedy's bed is upstairs. Right upstairs. Right upstairs. So is Mum's and Daddy's. So is D'onny's."

She came and leaned against him, as he had against Mr. Shawn. He held her tight.

He said, "In this home we've got a doggy. See our doggy. Here's his tail. Here's his ears. Here's his mouth. Deedy pat the doggy's paws."

She patted with one hand, clinging to Johnny's shoulder with the other.

"D'onny home?" she asked.

"Sure. I'm home. Deedy's home. Doggy's home. Want D'onny to sing to you, Deedy?"

"D'onny sing."

She crept into his lap. He could feel her breathing against him. He held her foot in his hand. He sang the last verse because he liked the last verse best.

· 69 ·

" 'Faith of our fathers, we will love
'Both friend and foe in all our strife
'And preach thee, too, as love knows how
'By kindly word and virtuous deed . . .' "

He sang it over and over.

When their mother opened the door she called softly: "Jack. I want you to look here. Isn't that a picture?" Their father, across her shoulder, said, "Quite a picture."

Johnny smiled at them. Deedy crept toward them. Her mother caught her up.

"All happy now, precious? You had a nice time with Big Brother? Well, now come have your supper. I'll bet you're hungry."

"Bet Big Brother's hungry too," his father said.

And Johnny was. He suddenly realized that he had never been so hungry. He ate enormously. His mother said she did not know where he put it all. His father said boys had places.

While his mother was putting Deedy to bed, he finished writing his sentences.

I have a little sister. I have a little sister.

We have come to live in town. We have come to live in town.

It was not hard to write them now. It was

easy. Almost too easy. Perhaps he was not writing well enough. He tried to draw each letter as if it were a picture.

Christmas is a week from Sunday. Christmas is a week from Sunday.

Why, that was not a long time. A week from tomorrow. Tomorrow he would go to Sunday School. Then in a week it would be Christmas Day. He began to wonder what he would get for Christmas. He had not thought of it before. It did not matter how expensive bicycles were. He did not want a bicycle.

When his mother came downstairs he showed her the papers.

She said, "Johnny, they look fine. You were good to go back and finish them. It was a big job for you to do. Maybe I shouldn't have given you so much."

"Aw, it wasn't much," he boasted. "I can write good now, can't I, Mum?"

"I call it very nice writing," she said, "for a boy nine years old. Don't you, Jack?"

"For nine—or ninety," his father stated, after one quick glance.

"Now hear me spell, Mum?"

"Well—I ought to do the dishes next."

"Oh, hear him spell," his father said. "And

have it over with. We'll do the dishes after he's in bed."

So she asked him to spell boy, must, try, well, go, all, hard, very, good, week, come, and live. Then she asked him to spell school, study, teacher, mother, father, little, sister, and town. Even Christmas and Sunday. And he spelled every one right the first time, not forgetting capitals.

"Well, Johnny Lee!" she exclaimed. "I think that's wonderful. I don't believe but Miss Besse would too. You see, you can do it if you try, can't you? After this, will you try at school, too, Johnny?"

He nodded.

My mother wants me to try hard.

He had tried, but he would try again. Maybe it would work. Anyway he would try again.

" ' . . . *In spite of danger, fire, and sword . . .* ' "

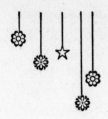

Sunday

3

*I*T was certainly going to be a white Christmas.

It had snowed heavily in the night, but the big snowplow had been out before daybreak, clearing the streets, and before nine o'clock the sidewalk plow had gone through the village. The pattern was that of a broad band of Hamburg insertion, and two narrow bands, all separated by ruffles of lace, running around the hem of the smooth white cambric petticoat which was the lawns before the houses and the outlying fields which narrowed with distance as if fitted to a woman's waist.

Johnny's father, used to waking early, had finished breaking his path before the sidewalk plow went past, and was there, leaning on his shovel, to wave and grin at the driver and shout, "What did you do, oversleep?"

Johnny, at the window, had seen and heard him.

He wished then that he had not had to take a bath. He wished he had been dressed and down there, to shovel and wave and grin with his father. But his mother had said the snow was too heavy for him; and besides, he had to get ready for Sunday School.

It was still snowing when Johnny left the house, but it did not seem like a stormy day. The sun was not far behind the clouds. Big soft white flakes drifted down through a haze of the faintest possible shade of lemon color. It was not cold, and there was no wind. Great masses of the night's snow clung to the edges of house and garage roofs like the loose folds of warm shawls, and sometimes slid off as ladies might drop them, with grace and luxurious abandon. The spruce and cedar trees in dooryards were decorated for Christmas with a triangle of silver crowning each branch and every tip punctuated by a slender icicle.

Johnny walked fast at first but when he found there was no one else but him the whole length of the street, he moved more and more slowly.

Everything was so still. Everything was so big. And all the bigness was so peaceful.

He could even stare at the houses because no one seemed to be awake in any of them. Smoke came curling out of their chimneys and turned dark gold in the lemon-yellow air. The windows looked at without seeing him. The doors were like quiet mouths. He walked slowly along a narrow band of Hamburg insertion, sometimes stopping to touch the lace with his mitten or to catch a falling flake and see how long it would live with him. When it died, it seemed to go with pleasure and he closed his hand over its going, feeling it melt sweetly into the palm of his hand. He thought God must do that for people when they went—look down at them with tenderness, wait a little in interest and pity because they did not know what He was going to do, and then close his Hand over them gently, taking them into Himself.

The church bells began to ring at each end of the village. The first peal was soft, like a mother speaking to wake her child. The next was louder. The two tones ran to meet each other, and blended.

It was like Mr. Shawn and Johnny singing together.

Louder . . . Louder . . . Louder.   Loud and strong and true.

Now it was God calling. The village was shaken by the reverberation. Johnny was alone in a strange new country, but it was a friendly country. He was not afraid. He answered.

He tipped his head back, letting the snowflakes fall on his lips and nose and eyes, and, looking up through them, said cheerfully, "Good morning, God!"

He heard doors opening behind him, but he was ahead.

He had reached the Square.

To the right he saw the tall, gilded spire of the Baptist Church where he had gone several times with Linda, but it meant nothing to him now. Linda would not be there. Linda was far away, in her grotto.

To the left was the square bell-tower of the Methodist Church. That was where he had gone a great many times long ago, and had felt lost and lonely. But it would not be like that today because Mr. Shawn was there. And now he had God.

Johnny turned left.

He passed the postoffice. Its green shades were drawn. He passed the stores, the bank; all closed. He passed the school, but he did not look at it. He did not have to go to school today. Today he was going to church. Mr. Shawn was there, and God was going with Johnny. Perhaps He would come back with Johnny too, and stay to go to school with him tomorrow. That should make a great difference. He had never been there before; or if He had, Johnny had not known it.

" 'We have come to live in town,' " thought Johnny, writing the words on the seam of his trousers. "This is my town now."

He walked along confidently and when he came to the church did not hesitate, but went straight in at the big door.

Mr. Shawn stood just inside, as Johnny had known he would.

A light broke quickly over his face. His hair gleamed like the living-room fire. He held out his big, warm hand.

"Good morning, Johnny!"

It was as if God replied to Johnny's greeting in a glad voice.

"You're early. I believe you're the first one here for Sunday School. That's good, too, because I can go with you to your teacher."

They started down the vestry stairs together.

"I'll tell you what I've made up my mind, Johnny. After hearing you sing yesterday, I think you should be in Mrs. Curtis' class. Maybe you won't know many of the boys in that class, because she has the ones who are in the fourth grade at school, and I believe you're in the third, aren't you? But you read so well, I think you will be more interested in what Mrs. Curtis' class is doing than you would be in Miss Kimball's group where you used to be. And you'll soon get acquainted, son . . . Oh, there you are, Mrs. Curtis. This is Johnny Lee. He would like to join your class today."

Johnny looked at Mrs. Curtis' blue serge skirt. It was broad and long.

"That's fine," said a quick voice. "Glad to have you, Johnny. I think I've seen you at school."

"Yes'm," said Johnny. "I'm in—Miss Besse's room."

He thought perhaps he was going to be sick. He had the same feeling he had on schoolday mornings. He had heard Mrs. Curtis' voice on the playground and in the halls.

"Step lively there, children." . . . "Come, come, now, David! You know you're not allowed on those steps!" . . . "Nancy, keep on your own side!"

He had seen Mrs. Curtis through the glass door of the fourth grade room. She was always very busy. She took quick steps, for such a big woman. Everything about her was quick. Even her eyes snapped. It was much quieter next door than it was in Miss Besse's room. He remembered that Linda had said Mrs. Curtis was nice, but he had often wondered what Mrs. Curtis did to make people in the fourth grade so quiet. A boy had told him once that she kept a strap in the closet, and that was why she never sent people to the principal as other teachers did.

"But he reads better than most third-graders," Mr. Shawn was saying. "I think he would like that project your class is working on, Mrs. Curtis. And he has a remarkable voice for singing."

"Well," said Mrs. Curtis, "we'll be glad to give him a try. We certainly need a good singer. Our row usually sounds like a flock of crows, and I caw worse than anybody."

Mr. Shawn laughed.

"Well, I'll leave Johnny with you then," he said, "and get about my business upstairs. I hope you'll enjoy yourself, son. In fact, I know you will."

Johnny was alone with Mrs. Curtis.

"We might as well sit down," she said briskly, "and rest our feet and hands. Some of the rest of my boys are coming downstairs now. I'll know the sound of their steps when they're tramping over my grave. Every blessed one of them. This is our row, Johnny. Take up all the room you can. Looks better. Class will probably be small today. Snowballing's good."

She pushed him ahead of her and settled herself, opening her fur collar, straightening the seams of her gloves, fixing her hat with quick motions.

Following her hands, he stole a glance at her face. It looked exactly as it did through the glass door at school.

She bent sidewise toward him, keeping her eyes front, and whispered, "Am I all right, Johnny? Do I look as if I'd hold together 'til meeting's over?"

"You look nice," he whispered back. "You look awful nice."

He was surprised. She did look nice.

"Flatterer!" she scoffed.

Her eyes snapped. She reached briskly for hymn books and passed them to boys pushing past her or coming in from the other side.

"Get ready," she told them. "In a minute here we're going to sing. We're going to sing like sixty."

Two or three boys tried to sit down between Johnny and Mrs. Curtis but she did not make room for them.

"Move along," she said. "Move along."

The row filled up. Soon it had all it would hold. They were all squeezed together.

Johnny had never seen before the boy who sat beside him; a tall boy with sandy hair and glasses who said nothing and kept his eyes on the hymn book. From three seats down the boys who had thrown the snowballs from across the street the day before bent forward to stare at Johnny. One of them demanded, "What you doin' here?"

Johnny did not answer. His shoulder was behind Mrs. Curtis's shoulder.

She answered for him.

She said, "Sit up straight, Wally Stewart. You'll grow taller. Quiet now, everybody. Mr. Richmond is about to begin."

Out of the corner of her mouth she whispered to Johnny, "Can you breathe? I'm just like the old woman in the shoe, here. Only I hope she wasn't as fat as I am." She added, "Keep quiet, Almira Curtis!"

Johnny giggled, and she said, "Sh-h-h," quite loudly, with her eyes fixed on the old man who stood now on the platform.

Upstairs the organ was playing. It sounded far away and majestic. It sounded as if God had withdrawn to his heaven, where all was right and beautiful, but rather too grand for a small boy. God and Mr. Shawn had left Johnny with Mrs. Curtis who was big and quick and snappy-eyed and could make Johnny laugh.

"We'll open our program this morning," said Mr. Richmond, "ahem—by singing Number 148. Shall we all stand?"

They stood. Mrs. Curtis held one corner of a hymn book and Johnny held the other.

"Sing loud," she whispered. "Drown me out."

He threw his head back and sang loud.

He looked across the aisle at the boys sitting where he had used to sit, with Miss Kimball. There were only three and he knew all of them. They were in Miss Besse's room at school. Kenny Schultz, Pete Barker, and Tarb Mac-Donald. They were taking pokes at one another. Miss Kimball moved in between Pete and Tarb. A minute later she reached across and shook Kenny a little by the shoulder. She looked as if she thought they were being very silly. Johnny thought so too.

He looked down the crowded row in which he sat and saw that all the boys were singing lustily, even Wally Stewart.

He was glad to be with boys who sang when it was time to sing.

He sang louder than ever.

Then Mr. Richmond prayed and at the end they all said the Lord's Prayer together. It was different from saying it at school. There were so many voices, and upstairs the organ was playing, people were singing, like a heavenly accompaniment to the words.

"A-men," said Mr. Richmond. "Stand, boys and girls."

The piano struck up a march. Mrs. Curtis strode out into the aisle and Johnny followed her proudly up the long aisle and across the back of the room and through a doorway, as if flags were flying and bugles blew. It was not at all as it had used to be when he straggled after Miss Kimball.

"Now," she said, as soon as the door was closed behind the last boy in the line, "let me just get these duds off."

She put her hat and gloves on the window-sill, and smoothed her hair back. She looked ready for business.

"Boys, this is Johnny Lee. He'll learn your names fast enough. Johnny, we've just finished studying about where Jesus lived when he was your age, more or less, and where he went with his folks for the Feast of the Passover. They were Jews, you know. That shows you the kind of people the Jewish are. A great race. Fine heads, big hearts, and a faith strong enough to last for thousands of years through more trials and tribulations than bear thinking on, almost."

" 'Faith of our fathers living yet,' " said Johnny. " 'In spite of dungeon, fire and sword.' "

"Right, " said Mrs. Curtis. "Where he lived and where they went for the feast is all on that map Carl made, over there. It's a fine map. Nice letters on it. Clear as a bell. Wally made the pictures. Wally's our artist. You go over and study it, Johnny. You'll see where Jesus rode his donkey and where he stayed behind at the temple and asked questions of the teachers. Jesus wanted to learn things.

"Now we are going to try to figure out where a boy would ask questions today. A boy in our time. A boy who wanted to learn as much as he could about everything that is important. We'll need a map for this too. Get your drawing paper, Carl. Put our state on the northeast corner of it—up here—and somebody'll tell you where to make a star for our town. He might as well start from our town because he is a boy like you. You boys want to know things too. What do you want to know about, Slim?"

Slim wanted to know about machinery. Especially automobile machinery. About engines and cauter-pins and piston rings.

Where would he go to find out things like that, Mrs. Curtis asked. The boys decided on Detroit.

"That's on Lake Erie," said Mrs. Curtis. "Draw in your Great Lakes, Carl. You know how they look. In general. Middle top. That's right. Now how'll Slim get there? On a donkey?"

They all laughed.

"Not on a donkey? Why not?"

"Because he hasn't got a donkey?" Johnny asked; and added, "Has he?"

They all laughed again, except Mrs. Curtis.

She said, "That's one reason. Too bad, too. Slim would have a lot of fun with a donkey. But he couldn't get to Detroit on one very well. Why not?"

"Too slow," someone said.

"That's right. A donkey is slow, and Detroit is a long way off. How would he go?"

"By plane," cried several. "Draw in a plane for Slim, Wally."

"All right if there isn't a storm. What if the planes are grounded, and Slim's bag is all packed?"

"By train!"

"Or by car."

"Slim hasn't got a car either."

"Maybe he could use his father's."

"You don't know my father," said Slim glumly. "He wouldn't let me go at all. If he knew it. Jesus's folks didn't know it."

"They took him there in the first place. He just stayed behind."

"He didn't mean to, did he, Mis' Curtis? He just forgot."

"I think so."

"His folks was kind of mad, though."

"My folks would be mad."

"Mine wouldn't."

"Well, I don't know. Maybe mine wouldn't."

"Johnny, put in the railroad track. Arnold, you draw the road. Wally'll put the car on the road and the train on the track. We'll get Slim there one way or another. If that's where he wants to go. Because machinery is very important in the world today. There are a lot of things God depends on us to do, now we have machinery, that He didn't expect in Jesus's time. And we need boys like Slim to learn to make it for us and keep it in good order."

Johnny was drawing the railroad track very neatly and carefully. It took a long time. Detroit must be a long way off. He had never heard of Detroit before.

"See what a big country this is," Mrs Curtis said, "when we start travelling over it. Still it's a small part of the world. See, a map the size of this one we're making now shows all the towns in the part of the world Jesus knew about. This new map wouldn't have room for a fraction of the towns and cities in just our own country. It will take a great many maps of this size just to give an idea of the world that you boys are going to have to know about and help take care of when you're grown up. So we certainly can't depend on donkeys for getting around over it, can we? But the place to begin to learn the things we want to know is right in our own town. Ink in the name of it, Tony; and Detroit on Lake Erie too. Because Slim wants to know where that is, when he is old enough to travel that far alone . . . Now what does somebody else want to know about?"

They took Arnold to Texas to learn about drilling for oil; Wally to California to study airplane design; Carl to Washington to find out about the government; Tony to a Wyoming cattle ranch; Lloyd to a university where he could do experiments in a laboratory; Ernest to New York to learn merchandising . . .

Johnny kept on carefully making the tracks over which they would travel. West and south, south and west from the northeast corner.

"My land," Mrs. Curtis exclaimed. "There's the piano starting again. Who'd believe an hour would go so fast? We've only had time to find out what half of you would like to learn and where you might go to learn it. Well, we'll just have to wait to find out about the rest of you. And then will come the most interesting part. Then we'll have to try to figure out whether we think Jesus would consider it important for him or his friends to learn these things if they were the boys of today, and whether there are other important things we hope other boys will be learning while you are learning these."

"Now, here's your text for next week. A copy for each. Keep it with you. Read it over when you can. Think about it. Use it. You don't need to memorize it. But some of you will. I can't sit with you for the closing hymn today, so show Mr. Richmond it doesn't make any difference whether I'm there or not. He thinks I keep you in order. I know better. Class dismissed."

As she was pulling on her hat she noticed that Johnny was still there.

"Gracious," she said. "They need you to help sing."

"I'm going," Johnny said.

But still he stayed.

"I've got to run upstairs and walk home with my mother," Mrs. Curtis said, "or she'll start right out alone. Good days I let her. But in a storm I don't think it's right. She could fall and break a hip, like anybody else, but she doesn't think so."

"Have you got a mother?" Johnny asked.

"I should say so. Stubbornest old lady you ever saw. Just like me."

"If you've got a mother, you can't be very old. Are you?"

"Old enough. Why?"

"I mean—they said you might be too old to teach. At school. Next year."

"Pshaw," said Mrs. Curtis. "They can't keep me out of school next year unless they put me in jail. Now run along, Johnny. And sing!"

She gave him a little push, and he went. But he did not sing.

Mr. Richmond had announced that the pulpit flowers had been donated, today, to the Sunday School. He believed there were enough for every child to have a blossom to take home to his mother as her first Christmas gift.

Each teacher, beginning with the teacher of the littlest ones, was to go forward, call the names of her pupils who were present, and present the blossoms. After the primary classes, all the girls' classes would be called, and then the boys'.

When Johnny took his seat, the small children were already standing with their flowers in their hands. The huge basket of brilliant red carnations seemed hardly to have been touched.

Now the third grade girls were going forward, one by one. Johnny recognized Nancy Bennett, Gloria Nash with her yellow curls, Joyce Mathes in a green coat with a leopard plush collar. He wished Linda were there. Linda would look prettier than any of them. Linda would like to take a red carnation home to her mother. And Linda, on her way back to her seat, would smile at Johnny.

But they did not send the Sunday buses any more.

The fourth and fifth grade girls . . . The sixth and seventh grade girls . . . The Junior High School girls . . .

"Gosh," muttered Wally. "They're most gone. All the best ones are gone. Why do darned old girls always have to be first?"

"Sh-h-h," whispered Johnny.

He was thinking of what Mrs. Curtis had said.

"Shut up," growled Wally. "Who set you up anyway, and never cropped your ears? I'll fix you, when we get out of here!"

Johnny tried not to hear what Wally said. He tried not to be afraid. He tried to put his mind on the carnations. He tried to imagine his mother's face when he brought in her first Christmas gift. A real flower. A real, living flower, in December. A flower that smelled sweet . . . He thought she would cry, "Oh, Johnny!" and sniff it and hold it out for Deirdre to sniff, but not let her take it, because she might break it. Then he would bring the thin green glass vase, and they would run water into it from the faucet, and then they would put the flower in it, and carry it into the living-room. His mother would put it in the center of the white lace mat.

His father would say later, "Where did this come from, Marge?"

And she would say, "Johnny brought it to me."

Surely the flowers would last. There were quite a few left . . .

"Miss Kimball next, please," Mr. Richmond said.

Miss Kimball hurried forward, her crisp veil going in and out with her breath. She was very thin and bent forward as she walked. She turned quickly, as she reached the platform, and found that Pete and Tarb were already wrestling on the bench where she had left them.

"Peter Barker," she called sharply.

Pete fell over Kenny's out-thrust foot. He picked himself up and gave Kenny a punch. He went down the aisle and took his carnation.

"Tarbell MacDonald," Miss Kimball had already called.

As the two boys met, Pete hit Tarb with the carnation. Tarb ducked and grinned.

"Kenneth Schultz," said Miss Kimball, in haste and desperation.

"Ah," said Mr. Richmond kindly. "Ah—I'll just sit with those young men of yours, Helen, while you read Mrs. Curtis' attendance sheet. She was obliged to leave early. You're—ah—handier with flowers than I am."

He did not say that he was handier with boys than she, but Pete, Tarb, and Kenny became suddenly models of good behavior. They sat quietly beside Mr. Richmond with angelic faces.

Miss Kimball peered through her veil at Mrs. Curtis' list. How long it was! At least three times as long as hers! What did Almira Curtis do to bring so many boys regularly to Sunday School? Her own were always dropping out. Her room had not had the attendance banner for months. She wondered if Almira brought something for her boys to eat. It was against the rules, but you could never tell about Almira . . .

She looked at the names on her list.

The first one was John Lee.

John Lee. John Lee. Johnny Lee . . . Why, he used to be in her class. He should be in her class now. He used to come down from the country on the bus. Then he had changed over to the Baptist Sunday School. Her brother's wife had told her about it, at the time. Miss Kimball had not been able to imagine why. Now he was back here today. He was one of the changeable kind nobody could depend on, apparently. And he was on Mrs. Curtis' list instead of hers. That just showed that Mrs. Curtis was doing something in her room which attracted wanderers.

"Carl Crawford," Miss Kimball said, passing over Johnny's name because she could not bring herself to say it.

Carl went down the aisle.

Johnny counted the carnations. He could see six across the front of the basket. Surely there were more behind the ferns.

"Wallace Stewart," read Miss Kimball, snatching up the flowers and handing them out. "Antonio Watkins. Leonard Mitchum. Lloyd Keyes. John Lee. Arnold Nash . . ."

Mrs. Curtis' boys were coming and going swiftly. Pupils who had their flowers were becoming restless, especially the little ones. The older girls slipped on their coats. The pianist was taking her place at the piano. Sunday School was nearly over for another week. It was time to go home to dinner.

Probably no one heard Miss Kimball say to Johnny, "Why don't you get your flowers at the Baptist church, young man?"

No one but Johnny.

He had already put out his hand. He stood below her, blinking . . .

Perhaps she did not mean to keep the flower from him. Perhaps he could have had it if he had reached a little higher.

But he turned and stumbled back up the aisle. Arnold Nash took the carnation Miss Kimball was holding, and she reached for another.

A few minutes later Mr. Richmond announced the closing hymn but Johnny did not
sing it.

Johnny was not there.

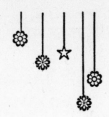

Monday

4

I DO believe it's going to make all the difference in the world," said Marge to herself, "his not having to go on that old bus."

She could not remember another school morning in two years when she had not been obliged to call Johnny at least three times before she heard him moving about in his own room, and after that to run upstairs and hurry him down, to remind him to wash, to urge him to sit down at the table and to get up from it. But today when she called, he answered "Okay, Mum," in a clear voice. A minute later she heard water running in the bathroom. When he came downstairs, the cuffs of his shirt were buttoned, his suspenders were straight, his face was scrubbed clean and shiny, and his hair was combed.

"My, Johnny! How nice you look!" his mother said, smiling.

He slid into his chair, tucked his napkin inside his collar, and picked up his spoon. He did not smile back at her, but perhaps it was too soon to expect a school-morning smile. She guessed that he had something on his mind—something important to him—but she did not feel that it was an unpleasant thing. His eyes were big, but not altogether sad. There was a kind of purposefulness in them; almost a gleam of hope.

"What you thinking about, Johnny?" she asked curiously.

"Nothing," Johnny answered.

They both knew that was not true. A boy says "Nothing" only because he is unable to say more.

He ate part of his egg, a few bites of bacon, half a slice of toast. It was not much, but it was more than usual, and he did it without dawdling, without pausing to rub his stomach uneasily or to rest his head on his hand.

He said, "That's enough, Mum. I'll go brush my teeth."

She was too astonished to ask him to try to eat more. He had never before brushed his teeth without being told.

"I do believe," she thought, "it's going to make all the difference in the world, his not

having to go on that old bus . . . I'd like to
know what he's got on his mind."

She saw no reason at all to be worried until
she noticed that it was half-past eight and he
had not yet come downstairs. School began at
quarter of nine.

She called, "Johnny! It's half-past eight."

"Okay, Mum."

"School begins in fifteen minutes."

"I know it."

Five minutes later she called again.

"What are you doing, Johnny?"

"I'm—in the bathroom."

"Well, hurry up. You mustn't be late the
first morning you have to get yourself to
school."

"I won't be."

In three minutes she called again.

"Johnny Lee! You've got just seven minutes
to get to school."

"I'll make it, Mum. I'll make it." This time
there was a note of desperation in his voice.

She wanted to go up, but intuition told her
it was better not to. She moved aimlessly back
and forth across the small kitchen, watching
the clock, watching other children hurry along
the street.

"Oh, dear," she thought anxiously, "now

· 103 ·

there isn't a bus driver, am I going to have to take him to school? I can't. I can't leave Deir. And if I have to get her ready and take her, he'd be so late I don't know what they'd say. I wish Jack was home. He'd see—"

At exactly nineteen minutes of nine the bathroom door opened, Johnny came clattering down the stairs, stepped into his boots, grabbed his jacket and lunchbox from her, and ran out saying "Bye, Mum" without turning his head.

Sighing with relief, she watched him race down the street faster than she had ever seen him move. There was not another child in sight. All the others must be safely on the school grounds already.

She looked at the clock. Eighteen of. He was disappearing. He probably would make it, as he had said he would. But what did it mean?

She shook her head. She could not think about it any longer, for Johnny's clattering had wakened Deirdre.

Johnny had calculated perfectly. He reached the school grounds as the last of the second graders were filing in past Mr. Sturtevant. Panting, he wriggled in between two third grade girls.

"You were almost LATE," said one of them accusingly.

"Where you been, hayseeder?" muttered Wally Stewart, from behind. "Why don't you try gettin' into the fourth grade line here, like you did at Sunday School? I was layin' for you, long as I could, and I will be again, don't you forget it. I'll get you yet!"

"Silence in the lines," said Mr. Sturtevant in his dry, cold voice. "Third grade, pass!"

"I'll tell Mrs. Curtis," thought Johnny. "If I have to, I'll tell Mrs. Curtis."

It was fine to know that there was someone, at last, whom he could tell about things other boys said or did to him, if they were bad enough, if he had to. There never had been anyone before. It was no use to tell his mother for she could not do anything about it and would only worry; and he did not dare to tell his father because his father would say he should stand up for himself, show a little spunk, fight his own battles. Only Linda knew what he had been obliged to take from other boys, and she did not know all of it. At school boys and girls were separated on the playground. Linda knew what she had seen, but he had never told her the rest. What she did know had made her cry with helpless rage, because Johnny was small and could not hate, and she was a girl. Seeing Linda cry was worse than being hurt. He wanted Linda to be happy. Some day he would be so big that he would not need to hate; then he would take care of himself and Linda and she would be happy all the time.

He tried to catch sight of Linda by stretching his neck and peering ahead, but a teacher touched him with a ruler as he passed her, and he shrank into his place. He thought perhaps Linda had not come today. Perhaps she had caught cold playing in the ice.

"Move along," said Miss Besse. "Move along."

It was what Mrs. Curtis had said yesterday but it did not sound the same.

Then, as he was hanging up his jacket, he saw Linda sitting at her desk, bent over, taking off her overshoes. He felt much better. He started up the aisle—her aisle—with his lunch box in his hand. He thought that as he went by he would swing his lunch box against Linda and she would lift her head and look around at him. He would not speak, of course. Miss Besse did not allow speaking without permission, in the room. Anyway, he did not have anything he needed to say to Linda. He only wanted her to look at him.

"Johnny Lee!" said Miss Besse. "Your own aisle, please!"

She saw everything, he thought. She probably could see into Johnny. She saw that he wanted to make Linda look at him and because it was what he wanted it was what she did not want. But this time she did not have her way. For once, she guessed wrong. The minute Miss Besse said "Johnny Lee!" Linda's head flew up. She did not look at Miss Besse. She looked straight at Johnny, and smiled, and hunched her shoulders, lifting her eyebrows. He knew what that meant. It meant, "Mean old thing, isn't she?"

"Johnny Lee, take your seat," said Miss Besse. "Linda, I don't like your attitude."

Several children snickered.

Everyone knew that Johnny was Linda's boy friend. They had known it since subprimary. Many of them remembered how, in their first days at school, Johnny had wanted to play on the girls' side, to be with Linda. They might not have remembered it—because at that time none of them had realized there was much difference between girls and boys—if after they had seen him playing there with Linda for two days (a pair of strange children from up-country whom no one knew or noticed much) their teacher had not appeared around a corner on the third morning and said:

"Johnny, this has gone on long enough. You aren't a girl, are you? So why are you playing on the Girls' Side? Get over on the Boys' Side where you belong!"

If Johnny had grinned and ducked and run, they might not have remembered it.

But Johnny had stood still and said, "I want to play with Linda."

Miss Secord laughed, exchanging glances with other teachers.

"My, my," she said. "So young, too! Well, I'm sorry, but you can't play with Linda on the school grounds."

The other children gathered around. They liked to hear Miss Secord laugh. They laughed too.

She took Johnny by the shoulder and steered him around the building to the Boys' Side.

"There," she said. "See you stay here. It's the Rule."

Johnny stood staring at other boys chasing one another, pushing one another down, throwing hard balls at one another. Someone bumped into him. Someone hit him, said,

"You're It," and ran away. Johnny stood staring, until the bell rang.

"What's the matter with ya? Ya dumb?" a big boy asked, knocking off Johnny's cap.

The next recess Johnny went back to play with Linda.

"You can't play with her," the other children cried. "You're a boy! You're a boy! Get over on the Boys' Side where you belong!"

"You leave him alone," Linda told them savagely. "He can too play with me. He always plays with me. You shut up. I like him best of anybody. You leave us alone."

She put her arms around Johnny and kissed his cheek. She had never done that before.

"Missecor! Missecor! Johnny's on the Girls' Side. Linda's kissing Johnny!"

Miss Secord descended upon them.

She said, "Hush. That's tattling. But what are you here for, Johnny Lee? Didn't I tell you to stay on the Boys' Side? Now listen. I'm going to take you back there just once more. If you come over here again, do you know what will happen to you? Do you know what we do to a boy that goes on the Girls' Side? We decide he wants to be a girl, and we put a girl's dress on him and make him stay over here. Then do you know what the boys do—and the girls too? They call a boy like that a Sissy."

Johnny blinked. His first blink.

Miss Secord took him by his shoulder again.

"March yourself," she said. "If any teacher ever sees you over here again, you know what will happen. And NOBODY likes a Sissy."

The next morning Johnny felt sick when it was time to go to school. He never had before.

He never went on the Girls' Side again. He never again played with Linda at school. But everyone knew he was still Linda's boy friend because he stood across the line and watched her, or tossed a rubber ball back and forth across the line to her whenever they could escape the attention of the others long enough. It was a popular game with the others to snatch their ball and to drag Johnny and Linda in opposite directions, until they were out of each other's sight. Linda around the corner of the building or behind the hedge where the girls had to let her go before she bit their hands or broke their ankles with her kicking, Johnny submerged under a heap of squirming boys who tore his clothes and rubbed snow or mud on his face.

"I hate 'em. I hate 'em all," Linda said, over and over, as they rode home the bus at night. Don't you, Johnny?"

But that was Johnny's trouble. He could not hate.

". . . And preach thee too, as love knows how,
"By kindly word and virtuous deed."

He looked up now at Miss Besse, who stood behind her desk with the Bible in her hands. She looked determined.

"If you are all settled," she said, "please listen to me for a moment. This should be a very pleasant week for us all. It is the last week before Christmas. On Friday we shall have a Christmas party here in our room. If you work well until recess time, after recess we shall begin making decorations for the room and for the tree which will be delivered this afternoon. I am sure you will all enjoy that. Some time soon we shall exchange names, and each of you may bring a gift for the person whose name you draw. It must not cost over a quarter. That is a new rule which Mr. Sturtevant has made this year, and I think it is a very wise one. The value of a gift is not the amount of money you pay for it. Now I must ask you to remember that we must not neglect our work for pleasure. The work is to be done first, and well. I shall now read from the second chapter of the Gospel according to St. Luke . . . 'And it came to pass in those days, that there went out a decree from Caesar Augustus, that all the world should be taxed. . . .'"

Johnny listened and thought of Joseph and Mary going to Bethlehem to be taxed, and their baby being born; but it was not their home, and the three of them "returned into Galilee, to their own city of Nazareth."

Miss Besse's reading stopped there, but Johnny's thinking did not stop there. He thought of the child growing older and stronger, and becoming a boy who went up to Jerusalem for the Feast of the Passover and staying behind, when it was over, to listen to the wise men in the temple and ask them questions. He wondered how Jesus had dared to ask them questions. Jesus must have been a very brave boy. . . . He thought of the map at Sunday School which showed the way Jesus had travelled to the temple; and then of the map which showed the ways Slim, Arnold, Wally, Carl, and the other boys might travel to find out what they wanted to know. He wondered what he wanted to know, and where he would go to find it out. He made railroad tracks slowly and neatly on a wrinkled bit of paper. He knew the marks started from this town where he was now, but he could not see where they led to. He thought that if he kept on making marks, carefully, God would tell him where they were going.

"I am very much surprised," said Miss Besse distinctly, "very much surprised—that while the rest of us were praying, someone was playing with his pencil! . . . Singing books, please. Who would like to choose the first Christmas carol of the season? Debby?"

They sang carols, and, as he sang, Johnny pretended that he stood between Mr. Shawn and Mrs. Curtis.

Miss Besse thought, "That Johnny Lee has the best voice in the room."

But of course she could not say so.

They saluted the flag, and she noticed that Johnny stood as straight as any soldier and that he looked neater than usual today.

She thought, "If he hadn't acted the way he did when he came in, and diddled with his pencil during the Lord's Prayer, I'd think maybe we'd begun to make something of him at last. But it's probably only that now he doesn't come on the bus he's trying to look and act like the town boys. He'll be as fresh as the rest of them in a few weeks, I suppose."

She passed out workbooks for the arithmetic lesson and sent several of the best pupils to the blackboard to figure the problems. It did not occur to her to send Johnny because he was not a good pupil in arithmetic and, besides, she never sent Johnny to the blackboard. The second grade teacher had written in her report that almost every time John Lee was sent to the blackboard he just stood and looked at it, but did not write anything. If she stood over him and made him use his chalk, he cried. When she had tried everything else, she gave him the ruler. The next time after that he would not even leave his seat, but just put his head on his desk and cried. Miss Besse had resolved that she would let him stay away from the blackboard the whole year, and see how he liked that. Most of the children loved to use chalk, and she had too many problems already without trying to handle a crybaby in the third grade.

The assignment in the workbook was finished before recess. Miss Besse checked a few of the books while the children were on the playground and found them reasonably satisfactory. When the children came back, she passed out materials for making paper chains.

Linda Morris was very skillful with her

hands. Miss Besse, watching her at work, wished the fingernails were cleaner, and the hair of the bent head, but she tried not to be prejudiced against children who came from poor homes.

She held up Linda's chain and said, "Try to make one like Linda's. See? The edges she has glued down are perfectly even. She has used deep, bright colors which show up, and she has put the color on smoothly. There are no streaks."

The chain swung lightly from Miss Besse's decent, middle-aged finger.

Johnny looked at it with admiration. He was proud of what Linda had done. He looked at his own chain and saw that its colors were pale and streaked, that the places where the edges of the loops came together were not even. He asked for clean paper, chose crayons of a deeper, brighter shade, and began again. He had not finished his second chain when Miss Besse sent the collectors around.

"Slowpoke!" hissed Georgia Raeburn. "I've made three already. Give me the one you have got done, stupe."

She snatched the pale, streaked chain with the uneven edges, and tossed it on the growing heap on Miss Besse's desk. Her skirts rustled as she switched back to her seat.

"Put your materials away," said Miss Besse. "Rise. Pass to the cafeteria."

Johnny saw Mrs. Curtis in the cafeteria.

She was the only teacher who sat with her grade at lunch. The other teachers had a table by themselves. There was a place for Mrs. Curtis at the teachers' table but she never used it. She was talking rapidly as the third grade filed in, and Johnny tried to hear what she was saying but her words did not carry beyond the fourth grade table.

"Gee, I bet Four's gettin' the devil," one third grader said to another. "Least, Miss Besse leaves us alone to eat."

Johnny was thankful for that, too. But he wished he were beside Mrs. Curtis. He knew now that whatever she was saying would be good to hear.

He passed quite close to her, with his tray, but she did not see him.

"I climbed a tree," she was saying. "I did, too! I was scared to death. You can do things when you're scared that you can't do any other time. It makes you strong."

Johnny thought about that all through lunch. Being scared had never made him feel strong. It made him feel weak. He wanted to ask Mrs. Curtis why that was.

He had tomato soup with the sandwiches he had brought from home. He did not like tomato soup, and when Tarb kept bumping his arm so that the soup spilled out of the spoon, he stopped trying to eat it. He munched his dry sandwiches and wondered if Mrs Curtis had ever really been scared and if it had really made her strong. He wanted to ask her about it. He wondered if he would dare to ask her, if he had a chance. Yesterday he would have dared to ask her anything; while she was with him, he could have asked her questions he could not even ask his mother, if he had thought of them. But she was not with him here. She was with the fourth grade.

He thought, "The priests weren't with Jesus. They were in their temples. Jesus went where they were, to ask them questions. Jesus dared."

He made up his mind that as soon as Mrs. Curtis left the cafeteria he would go upstairs and look through the door of her room. If she was inside, he would knock on the door, and she would call him in, and he would ask her about being scared and being strong. After that, maybe he would ask her whether it was wrong for him to want to play with Linda; and, if it wasn't, how he could play with Linda now that he no longer lived near her. After that, maybe he could ask her what he really wanted to know most today; that was whether he would ever see Mr. Shawn again, and whether he could ever be in her Sunday School class again, and if a person couldn't be a Methodist if he had ever gone to a Baptist church. He wanted to find out, too, why Wally was laying for him and why so many other boys in his grade and other grades laid for him, pushed him, knocked him down. He thought perhaps most of these questions were not important to anybody but him, and that surely Jesus had not dared to ask unimportant questions of the priests; but what Johnny needed to know was all mixed up and rolling over and over in his mind and he thought Mrs. Curtis would understand that he did not know which was important enough to ask about and which wasn't. Perhaps even Jesus asked some questions of the priests which did not seem important to them, but they took him in and let him stay three days, just because he was a boy trying to find out and they wanted to help him.

He began to feel braver than he ever had.

He thought, "She may not be in her room. If she isn't, she may be on duty on the playground. If she is on the playground I will ask her questions there. Unless she is on the Girls' Side."

He was the last third-grader to leave the cafeteria. He had tried to keep Mrs. Curtis in sight but in his haste to return his tray he tipped his bowl of soup and had to mop up the floor with paper towels. Then he had to wash his hands because they looked blood-stained.

When he reached the hall and started upstairs, Mrs. Curtis had disappeared.

Mr. Sturtevant, the principal, stood there, talking with a teacher. Without looking at Johnny, he put out a hand and stopped him.

Mr. Sturtevant finished what he was saying to the teacher.

Then he looked down and asked, "Where do you think you're going, young man?"

Miss Kimball had asked, "Why don't you get your flowers at the Baptist Church, young man?"

"To—to find Mis' Curtis," Johnny said, very low.

"Mrs. Curtis. Are you in Mrs. Curtis' grade?"

". . . No."

"No, sir."

"No, sir."

"Who is your teacher?"

"Miss Besse."

"I see. Well, Miss Besse's boys are outside this door. They are sliding on the ice. You go right along and slide on the ice until I ring the bell."

Mr. Sturtevant opened the door, pushed Johnny through it, and closed the door.

It was very cold outside. Johnny stood on the step, blinking.

He was not one of Miss Besse's boys, if she had any. Even though he was in the third grade, he was not Miss Besse's boy. But because he was not in the fourth grade, he was not one of Mrs. Curtis' boys either. He was nobody's boy, at school.

He stood on the step, blinking, until Kenny Schultz pushed him off.

"Wha's'a matter?" Kenny grinned. "Can't you slide? Can't you do nothin'? My father says why don't you never come ou'doors sence you moved down here. He said go get you but I tol' him you wouldn't come. I didn't tell him why, but I know. 'Cause you're yeller, you're yeller, you're yeller. You don't dare slide for fear you'll fall on your tail!"

Johnny did not answer. He moved away, trying to appear as if he had not heard. He did not run, at first, because he knew he would be overtaken. But when he saw Tarb come off the ice, and heard Wally shout, "Hold him for me, kids!" he ran. He ran as far as he could. He nearly reached the boundary of the Boys' Side. Sometimes if he was close to the Girls' Side, the boys let him go because of the teachers over there. As he felt them close in on his back and and begin to drag him down, he thought, "Somebody may stop them. Mrs. Curtis may be over there. If she sees them she will stop them—I guess."

But either she was not there, or she did not want to stop them. Nobody stopped them. They forced him down against the frozen ground. They pulled his hair. They stuffed snow inside his belt.

When they left him, he stood up slowly. He could not see. He could hear only faintly. What he heard was the bell ringing. He went in the direction of the eerie sound.

He was entirely alone.

Even back in his room, when he heard Linda saying hotly, "Miss Besse! Kenny and Tarb threw Johnny down in the snow! I saw 'em!" he was alone.

"Don't tattle, Linda," said Miss Besse. "Most of you are down in the snow most of the time."

"But they threw him down!"

"I don't see any bruises on him."

"Well, they're not on his *face*—"

Several children giggled.

"That will do, Linda," said Miss Besse, flushing. "Language workbooks, please. As I said this morning, when the workbooks are finished, we shall continue making preparations for Christmas. Not before. Page 43. At the top of the page, it says—"

Johnny groped for his pencil. He filled in blank spaces in sentences. Sentences with capitals and periods made him think of the sentences he had written on Saturday.

My teacher helps me all she can. My teacher helps me all she can.

He thought once more of Mrs. Curtis. Tears came to his eyes. He blinked them away. He had been to the Feast, but he had not stayed at the temple. The priests had not noticed him at all. After the Feast they had gone inside and locked the temple doors. His family had travelled homeward, left him behind, and he was alone. It was desert all around and the sand was cold because the sun had gone down.

"That is all," said Miss Besse. "Assistants, collect the books and pass out the materials for making paper candles. The prettiest candles will be pasted on our windows. The tree will not be here this afternoon, I understand, but you may see it when you come into the room tomorrow morning."

There were no trees where Johnny was, and would not be. He drew and colored a candle. It would not be one of the prettiest ones. This did not matter. His hand trembled as he cut it out.

As Miss Besse passed his desk, he mumbled, "May I get a book?"

"What did you say?" she asked, turning in surprise.

He repeated the words, with difficulty.

"Yes," she said. "But quietly. The others are interested in Christmas."

No one looked up as he tiptoed to the book shelf. Not even Linda. She was on the far side of the room and her head was bent over the beautiful candle Johnny knew she was drawing.

He took the first book his hand touched, and crept back to his seat.

It was a good book. It carried Johnny out of third grade, out of the town, even out of the time in which he had been born, as good books often did, and as only books and music ever had.

It picked him up, wafted him into the middle of another century than his own, and set him down on the bank of the Mississippi River. When he looked at himself he saw that his feet and legs were bare, his shirt was old and soft, his straw hat was broad and ragged. His name was Huck and he smoked a corncob pipe. He had no family. He did not have to go to school. He was alone and he liked it. He was thinking of floating down the river on a raft . . .

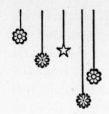

Tuesday

5

*M*iss Besse sniffed appreciatively as she entered her room.

She had cleaned it herself the afternoon before. The janitor was no more thorough in his cleaning than most men. She bought a powder for the floor which both disinfected and deodorized as she swept—or so the label said—and a polish for the desks which cleaned as it polished. She bought these materials out of her own small salary and used them at least once a week. Last night she had been at it, a towel around her head and a sweater on, windows wide open, until after five o'clock. Then she had allowed the big boys to bring in the spruce tree with which they had been waiting, impatiently, in the hall. She had a corner cleared for it. The tip nearly reached the ceiling. It was a well-shaped tree, and she was pleased with it. After that she had pasted the prettiest candles on the windows, and drawn Christmas designs and greetings with colored chalk on all the blackboards.

She had been late home to supper but it was worth a few scowls from her landlady to know that her room would be gay, ready, and in perfect order the next morning.

It was not only that; it was also fragrant with the smell of spruce which had been spreading through it all night.

She put a pile of workbooks on her neat desk and hung her coat in the tidy closet.

It was still early. The bell would not ring for ten minutes. The children were not allowed above the basement until after the bell rang.

She sat down at her desk and opened a workbook. It had been corrected. She had no work to do, but she wanted to appear busy if one of the other teachers should look in. She did not want a visitor. She wanted to enjoy this little time alone, before the children came in and began to absorb the clean fragrance, to replace it with the odor of their clothes, their hair, their grubby little fingers, and to nibble away at the neatness until it became like the shell of a squash from which mice have secretly gnawed out the inside.

But she was not to have this privilege.

An eighth grade girl knocked, with cafeteria

tickets, asking how many Miss Besse would need. The nurse sent word that two third graders had enlarged tonsils and she had received no reply from the notices she had sent their parents. What did Miss Besse know about the families of these two pupils? A member of the Christmas Seal committee stopped in to ask how many third-graders had taken seals to sell and how much money had come in; and would Miss Besse make sure that all money was collected and unsold seals returned by Thursday at the latest, as the principal was to announce on Friday which grade had proved to be the best sales force.

Miss Besse had all these records in books in her desk drawers, though little was known about the two with the large tonsils except that they came on the bus, had no telephone, one of them had seven brothers and sisters, and the other did not have the same last name as that of her mother.

The member of the Seal committee had not left the room when the children came tramping in. She was a former teacher, now married and—Miss Besse assumed—proud of her accomplishment, secure in her husband's protection, and quite certain that her own period of teaching had been highly successful from start to finish.

"I'll have the report for you Thursday afternoon, Mrs. Galway," said Miss Besse. "Several of the children have taken a second sheet of seals. Only three dollars and a few cents have come in so far, but—Kenneth, pick up your cap off the floor before it is trampled on! Girls, girls! Sh-h-h!"

"Goodness," murmured Mrs. Galway. "That closet is so crowded, Miss Besse. Isn't there danger of—well, creeping things?"

"I have forty-six pupils," said Miss Besse. "It's too many for the space. I'd like to push the walls out, but I can't."

She was afraid she had sounded crisp. She smiled, to soften it. She wished Mrs. Galway would go, but she had to be polite.

"How do you like our tree? Nice shape, isn't it? The children are looking forward to decorating it today. They made the paper chains yesterday—"

"Did they really like doing that? My subprimary class made paper chains. I shouldn't think third grade—"

"Some of them liked it," said Miss Besse. "Some of them made very nice ones, too. Better than subprimary children could. If you are going to visit us, Mrs. Galway, won't you take this chair? I have to call them to order now—"

"I should think so," said Mrs. Galway, wrinkling her dark little nose. "No, thanks, I can't stop. I still have Christmas shopping to do."

"So do I," thought Miss Besse. "And the chances are it will never get done. But hers will. And when she's tired from her Christmas shopping, she'll stop at the drug store for coffee and a cigarette. The only place I can have a cigarette in this town is in my room with the door closed."

"I know how that is," nodded Miss Besse pleasantly. "Well, I'll have the report for you Thursday afternoon. Good-bye, Mrs. Galway. Debby, open the door for Mrs. Galway. Now, children, I know you noticed our lovely Christmas tree, but—Deborah, close the door!—*but the way you have been behaving since you came into this room is not the way to win the pleasure of decorating a Christmas tree, or any other kind of pleasure!* What were you thinking of to be so noisy and kick your clothes around and push one another when Mrs. Galway was in the room? Were you trying to show off? Or did you think you could get away with it because we had a guest? I was ashamed of you. I was thoroughly ashamed of you. If that was what you wanted, you got it. This class will have no recess this morning. If that was also what you wanted, now you have it. If you cannot take off your outdoor things and go to your seats properly, you may stay in your seats. Sometimes I think you act younger than the children in the subprimary. It is very discouraging, especially just at this season of the year when grown-ups are trying to do more than ever for people of your age. Some of you, at least—"

She paused. The door was opening. A small boy with big eyes closed it softly and scuttled toward the coat closet. He did not look at Miss Besse nor at anyone in the room. He took off his boots, cap, and jacket with his head down and his shoulders hunched.

Miss Besse particularly disliked his manner. It suggested that he thought if he pretended to notice no one, no one would notice him. She thought of an ostrich with its head in the sand. She waited in silence, watching him try to find a hook on which to hang his cap and jacket. There was none. She watched him try to make them cling to other hanging caps and jackets. They slid off, taking other caps and jackets with them. She sighed audibly. Some of the children giggled. They watched him hang up the other caps and jackets and stand there, holding his own, with his eyes on the floor and his shoulders hunched. They watched him, finally, lay his jacket and cap on his boots, and tiptoe to his seat.

"Some of you, at least," resumed Miss Besse, "do not deserve what is being done for you at Christmas time . . . Johnny Lee, why were you late?"

Johnny swallowed and blinked.

"Stand up," said Miss Besse.

He stood up.

"Why were you late?"

"I—didn't start soon enough."

"Why didn't you start soon enough?"

He did not answer. She repeated the question.

Linda raised her hand.

"Put your hand down, Linda. Johnny?"

"Don't know," Johnny whispered.

"You don't know," said Miss Besse. She regarded him severely. "You will stay in at the morning recess. The others are staying in because they were noisy. You will stay in because you were late. I shall stay in for no good reason. We shall all suffer together. And this afternoon, John, you will take home a note to your mother informing her that school begins at quarter of nine. You may sit down now. Take positions for the opening exercises which must be brief today because we have already wasted much valuable time."

She read a few verses. They repeated the Lord's Prayer. They sang "America," and saluted the flag.

"Now, Group One, open your readers to page 47. Study the following two pages. Group Two, open to page 93 and read silently to page 97. Group Three, page 129. Debby Marshall, stand and read, please."

Group One was the slow group, Two the average, and Three the best readers. The numbers ran backward to prevent the children from guessing what they meant. Everyone knew who got the most votes in elections, who wore the best clothes, who passed in the neatest papers, who were the best ballplayers, who got E's on report cards, who made the prettiest paper chains; but that or why some children were given more advanced work than others was, insofar as possible, concealed.

Miss Besse did not question the system. The results of intelligence and placement tests came in to her at the opening of each school year and she divided the class accordingly, for each area of work. Some pupils were in Group

Three for reading and in Group One for arithmetic (Johnny Lee was one of these) and some the other way about, but the majority studied with the same group all day. It was rather like teaching three different grades, but she had developed the ability to keep them all busy, and, by this plan, she had an opportunity to concentrate on other shortcomings as well as that of not knowing that "house" and "home" are two different words or that three multiplied by four make twelve. She realized now that in the past she had spent undue time on slow children and let the quick ones do as well as they would, since they were always ahead of the others anyway.

The fact that Debby Marshall pronounced words well was not enough. She must learn to read with expression.

"Wait, Debby," said Miss Besse. "Let me read that sentence to you."

Miss Besse read as she wrote, beautifully, admirably.

"Now try it again, Debby."

Debby did much better on her second try. Miss Besse told her so. It was comforting to work with a child who responded to suggestion as Debby did.

Some of the others, however, reacted quite differently. Johnny Lee, for instance.

When she called on him, he began to read where he sat. He knew better than that.

"Stand up, John," she said.

He slid out of his seat slowly, provokingly, and began to read with one hand on his desk top. As he read, his hand moved gradually toward the far edge of his desk, until he was all but lying on it.

Miss Besse interrupted again.

"Stand up, John. Out in the aisle. Away from your desk. Don't touch anything but the book. Stand like a man. Now read to the bottom of the page."

When he finished, she went to the front of the room.

"Now, class," she said. "I want your comments on that recitation. What did you think of the way John read?"

"He read good," said Linda.

"Read well," said Miss Besse. "I was not asking you, Linda. You are not in this group. And he did not read well. He pronounced all the words properly but he did not read well. Why not? Donald?"

"He leaned on his desk."

"After he stopped leaning on his desk . . . Debby?"

"He said the words all in the same tone. All run together."

"That is true. He had no expression. What was another reason why the words ran together? Elizabeth?"

"He read too fast."

"That is right. I noticed something else about John's reading. I wonder if anyone else did."

Olivia Hemingway waved her hand wildly. "Olivia?"

"He put in words that weren't there at all!"

"Exactly. These are John's reading faults which we have been pointing out to him for months now. First, he does not stand properly. Second, he never changes the tone of his voice. Third, he reads much too fast. Fourth, he frequently puts in words which are not printed on the page. I cannot see that he has improved in his reading since the first of the year. He seems to be interested only in sitting down again as soon as possible. That is the reason, John, why you continue to get an F in reading. I am waiting and hoping for signs of improvement. Donald, continue, please."

It was a long forenoon without benefit of recess for either teacher or pupils.

Toward its close, Miss Besse passed back the language workbooks which she had corrected the night before, and directed the children to observe carefully the marks and comments which she had made in them.

This gave her ten minutes in which to find information about the two children with enlarged tonsils and to copy it off for the nurse. Her head ached. It seemed twenty-four hours ago that she had had her breakfast. Three more days after this before vacation! She wondered if by Friday night she would be capable of packing her bag and taking a train for her home in Connecticut. If she was, she knew that the minute she got there she would go to bed and sleep the clock around.

In Johnny's workbook there was written in red pencil: "All your mistakes are careless ones. You must spend more time on your work. Take no more books from the shelf this week."

A boy must try to do well. A boy must try to do well . . . All your mistakes are careless ones. All your mistakes are careless ones . . . My teacher helps me all she can. My teacher helps me all she can . . . First fault, second fault, third fault, fourth fault. I cannot see that he has improved. That is why he gets F . . . Take no more books from the shelf. Take no more books from the shelf. Take no more books from the shelf . . .

The Feast was over. The guests had departed. The temple doors were closed. And Huckleberry Finn had floated out of sight on his raft. Johnny was alone in the desert.

After lunch Miss Besse had the boon of a half hour in the teachers' room. She sat in a wicker rocker with her feet against the radiator and leafed through a new magazine bright with pictures of Christmas dinner tables, gift-wrapped packages, and toddlers hanging their stockings in chimney corners.

It occurred to her to wonder what happened to children between the ages of four and nine to make them change from the adorable cherubs they had once been into sly monkeys, proud peacocks, scared rabbits, and dull little grubs. Everyone loved subprimary children. They came with clean faces. They liked to wash their hands. They boasted of brushing their teeth. They did everything as well as they possibly could. They were eager to learn. They were responsive and affectionate. They were loyal to one another. In first grade they were less so; in second grade still less so; by third grade they were dirty and said they liked to be dirty, they were lazy, they cheated, they lied, they acted as if teachers were their mortal enemies, they kicked and mauled and told on one another. It seemed as if, the more that was done for them, the less civilized they became.

"Oh, well," sighed Miss Besse, "they aren't all so bad. They weren't all noisy this morning, but I punished them all. Now I'll reward them all, even those who don't deserve it. I'll give them a happy afternoon if it kills me. And if all Aunt Maude gets from me this year is a pretty card instead of a best seller."

She dropped her magazine into the rack, sprang to her feet, snatched her coat, and hurried uptown to buy forty-five fudgsicles.

Hurrying back with her arms full of paper bags, she caught sight of Kenny Schultz balancing perilously on the edge of the step which separated the school walk from the sidewalk. Pupils who did not go home for lunch were not allowed off the school grounds.

"Careful, Kenny," she said good-naturedly. "Stay where you belong, now. It's almost time for the bell."

"He don't dare step off," yelled Pete. "He

don't dare. He's got a dime and he don't dare spend it. He don't dare. He don't dare."

Miss Besse smiled and hurried into the building.

A few minutes later she told the third grade that they were going to have a nice afternoon together. First, they would each have a fudgsicle as an extra dessert; she hoped they had not eaten so much that they had no room for fudgsicles. They screamed that they had not, and she hushed them, still smiling. She said that when they had finished their treat, each one would draw the name of a classmate to whom he would bring a gift on Friday. Then they would hang their paper chains on the tree, and also the tinsel, the icicles, and the bells and balls and tiny silver trumpets which she had ready in her closet.

"Now stand and file past my desk," she said. "A fudgsicle for each of you."

She smiled at every pupil as he passed her, and nearly all smiled back.

But when they were seated, there was one fudgsicle left. She looked at it in surprise.

"Is someone absent?" she asked. "I thought everyone was present this morning."

"Kenny ain't come back," said Pete, rolling his eyes.

"Kenny? Where did he go?"

"He didn't go nowheres. He started, but Mr. Sturtevant see him an' made him come back and took him up to the office. He's gittin' a terrible lickin'."

"Oh, dear," said Miss Besse. "Oh, no, I don't think so. But he shouldn't have gone. And you shouldn't have dared him, Pete. I heard you dare him. Children, you all know it is the Rule that you must not leave the schoolgrounds during noon hour or recess unless you have special permission. Never, never do it . . . Well, we mustn't let this spoil our nice afternoon. Have your fudgsicles and then we'll draw names. I'll put Kenny's out on the window ledge so it won't melt."

The children lapped and sucked. Miss Besse refrained from making any suggestions about their manners.

"The subprimaries lap and suck," she thought, "and we think it's cute. I'll try to pretend I'm teaching subprimary this afternoon."

But it was not easy.

After a few minutes the door opened and Mr. Sturtevant pushed Kenny into the room.

"This boy of yours left the schoolground without permission," said Mr. Sturtevant to Miss Besse.

"St, st," said Miss Besse. "I am sorry to hear that."

"I have dealt with this offense," said Mr. Sturtevant. "If it is ever repeated, it will go harder with him."

He turned on his heel and went out.

Kenny stood by the coat closet, grinning. His face was red.

"What'd he do to you, Ken?" Pete asked.

"Never mind, Peter. Take your seat, Kenneth," said Miss Besse.

"Tell what he did. We want to know what he did. Come on, Miss Besse, let him tell," cried several girls.

Miss Besse knew they were getting out of hand. She tried to think of a way to get them back without spoiling the afternoon.

"Aw," Kenny said, "hit me with a ruler; that's all. Tried to make me cry. What'd he think? Nothin' but a little old ruler. He can't hit harder'n a fly. He says, 'Put out your hand.' So I did. 'Bend it back,' he says. So I bent it back. Then he hit it four, five times. 'Nuts,' I told him, 'that don't hurt none.'"

"Kenneth," said Miss Besse, rising, "I don't believe a word of it. And your grammar is terrible. Sit down and wash out your mouth with this fudgsicle. Come, children, finish your treat, and then we'll draw names."

They lapped and sucked again. Kenny sucked louder than any of the others.

Miss Besse began writing names on slips of scratch paper.

Suddenly Linda Morris cried, "Teacher! Look at Johnny! Johnny's—going to be sick!"

And he was.

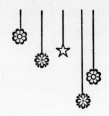

Wednesday

6

A NUMBER of people noticed Johnny Lee on Wednesday, though they did not think much about him at the time; not until later.

Mr. Shawn saw him from across the street, at about twenty minutes of nine, hiding behind the filling station which neighbored the school. He waved to Johnny, but the boy was looking in another direction. Mr. Shawn thought of crossing the street to speak to him, but supposed this would reveal the hiding place to Wally Stewart and Kenny Schultz who seemed to be the seekers in the game; besides, Mr. Shawn was on his way to visit a parish member who had suffered bereavement in the night. He thought he would call on the Lees late in the afternoon when Johnny would be at home; but this turned out to be impossible because the young widower was desperate in his grief and Mr. Shawn stayed with him until after the doctor came in the evening with sedatives to help the poor fellow get some rest. Then Mr. Shawn went home in need of food and sleep and his wife's gentle services.

Mrs. Curtis saw Johnny marching down the hall past her door, and thought, "How pale that child is. He didn't look that way Sunday. Must be coming on with something. If he were in my grade, I'd send him home."

But he was not in her grade, and passed from her sight.

Linda did not see him that day. Her mother was ill and she stayed at home to take care of her small brother.

Miss Besse saw him, of course, when she took attendance. She could prove that because she had marked him present, and she remembered later that she had noticed him especially because, after his illness the day before and his hour's rest in the nurse's room, she had thought he seemed well enough to walk home but might use that episode as an excuse to stay out the following day; or possibly he really had some virus thing, such as others had been having, though the nurse had said it could not be that because he had no fever, in fact his temperature was a bit below normal.

The nurse must have been right, for Johnny was in his place today and on time too. Like Mrs. Curtis, Miss Besse observed he was paler than usual, but that was natural after a stomach upset, and Johnny never had much color.

She drew attention to the beauty of the tree glittering in the morning sunshine, and allowed those pupils who had brought gifts to put them around the base.

"Don't they look mysterious!" she exclaimed. "Now who do you suppose that thick square one in the red paper is for? And this tiny little one in the white box! Good things sometimes come in very small packages, you know. Well, no one must peek at the labels. All will be revealed day after tomorrow. Do you think you can wait?"

There was a chorus of no's. She did not notice whether Johnny was one of those who said no. If he was, she thought later, perhaps he meant it. At the time she was not looking his way. She was concentrating on trying again to create the happy atmosphere which Kenny had punctured and Johnny, by being sick, had torn apart, the afternoon before.

"Well, we have to," she said smiling. "It will be good discipline for us. Today we'll open our morning exercises by singing "O, Little Town of Bethlehem."

She did not read from the Bible that day.

She asked the children to repeat only the prayer and the pledge to the flag. The rest of the exercise period she let them sing, and she was quite sure, later, that Johnny sang with the others. She thought he must have, because she knew he liked to sing and had a good voice; her book showed she always gave him G in music.

"Now," she said, "it is 9:10. Before we take up our school work,—how many of you have brought in money from the sale of Christmas seals? Mrs. Galway is going to collect our grade's contribution tomorrow afternoon. We hope it will be a big one. Remember that tomorrow morning you must bring in all money for the seals you have sold, and all the unsold seals you have. I must have the record exact for Mrs. Galway. If any of you have seal money today, bring it to the desk and I will check it against your name."

Ten or fifteen children gathered around her. Some had money tied into the corner of their handkerchiefs so securely that only adult fingers could wrench the knot apart. Some had it in purses they could not unclasp. Others had it in their pockets in pennies and counted each coin aloud as it came forth. Still others waved dollar bills from which fifty cents was to be taken, or forty cents, or seventy cents.

Children who had change coming back wanted to buy lunch tickets, wanted Miss Besse to keep the money for them until after school, dropped nickels which rolled under Miss Besse's feet where only she could retrieve them. Children who had not brought money pushed in upon the circle asking how many seals they had taken, how much money they had already brought in, if they must return seals which people on the street had given them money for but had not taken because they had plenty of Christmas seals at home. The subject of money had a fascination for them all, Miss Besse knew. The sight of it made their eyes widen and glisten. The poorest children, who usually were the quietest, had neither money to contribute nor questions to ask, but they hovered close, too, looking at the money, hearing it clink, jumping and staring, when a piece rolled across the floor, as if it might explode or set fire or, by chance, turn the whole room into Midas gold.

"Lunch tickets later," Miss Besse said over and over. "I only want seal money now. I have to keep the seal money straight for Mrs. Galway. Keep your change until later. Sit down, please, as soon as you have paid me. If you don't have seal money, don't come to the desk, children. Sit down until I have finished with this. Then we'll go on to other things."

She pushed back her hair distractedly. She could scarcely breathe. She wanted to ask someone to open a window but it was too much effort to make herself heard. She was not sure whether the same children still surrounded her or had been replaced by others. She was not sure she always gave the right change, or put it into the right hand. She was sure of only one point. That was that whatever was paid her for seals was accurately entered on her book and properly deposited in a box which had formerly held paper clips. She had to be sure of this because Mrs. Galway was coming the next day to collect.

At last no more money was being proffered. Miss Besse rose and told all the children to take their seats. She closed the paper clip box and opened the cafeteria box. She found relief in the plan of having each child who wanted a lunch ticket come alone to the desk. After that she took the change with which she was to serve as bank, and put it into envelopes which she kept for the purpose. She wrote the owner's name on each envelope.

"There we are," she announced valiantly. "Now in ten minutes I am going to ask you to write your spelling words. We won't spell orally first, as we usually do. So get out the lists I gave you yesterday and study them carefully. Then I'll pass out your spelling books."

She tidied her desk until they were all at work. She had raised a window a little but her throat still felt dry. She went into the hall to get a drink from the fountain, and hastily pushed a few bobby pins more securely into place. She had left her door open. She was out of sight of her desk, but she could hear every movement in the room and was certain that no one left his seat.

When she reentered the room three minutes of the ten still remained for studying. She sat down and looked again at the total of the third grade's Christmas seal sale so far. It was not large. Only $4.80. She was rather surprised. Perhaps a good deal would come in tomorrow. She opened the paper clip box and idly counted the contents . . . She counted them again, swiftly and anxiously . . . again, incredulously.

Then she stood up. Her chair slid back against the wall behind her with a thump.

She said "Children!"

They all looked up, startled.

"Children, there is a shortage of fifty cents in the Seal money box! I am positive there was no mistake in the total of what I put in there. I counted each pupil's money twice. I entered each amount by the name of the pupil who gave it to me, in my book. I am positive—and yet I shall give you the amounts to add. Turn over your spelling lists and put down these figures."

She read the figures aloud distinctly, adding them in her head. It came to $4.80.

While they added, she searched the top of her desk thoroughly, though she knew there was no loose money there; she had tidied it only five minutes ago.

"$4.80," called someone. "$4.80" . . . "$4.90" . . . "No, $4.80" . . . "I got $4.40."

Sighing, she asked all pupils who did not get a total of $4.80 to work the sum on the blackboard. Mistakes were rectified in all cases. $4.80 was the right answer.

"But," said Miss Besse, sadly, "there is only $4.30 here."

She counted it aloud, holding up each bill and piece of metal. She asked five different children to come to the desk, one by one, to count it.

"Two dollar bills. And fifty cents make $2.50. Three quarters makes $3.25. Six dimes make $3.85. Two nickels make $3.95. And the rest pennies. One, two, three, four, five, six . . . It comes out $4.30, Miss Besse."

"And I entered $4.80 in the book. I put $4.80 in this box. And now there is only $4.30 here. Fifty cents has disappeared. Fifty cents which we owe to Mrs. Galway. Fifty cents which was to make sick people well again. There has been no one in this room but us. I am the only one who has been out of the room. I did not take the fifty cents. I want all sick people to have a chance to be made well again. I am sure you all do, too. Perhaps the person who took the fifty cents did not realize what an important purpose it was meant for. You are all very young and none of you is sick. Please bring me the fifty cents and we'll say no more about it."

She waited hopefully. All their eyes were on her. But no one moved.

"I think," said Miss Besse, at last, very gently, "the pupil who took that fifty cents is sorry he did it now, and ashamed. He doesn't want the rest of us to know he did it. We can understand that, can't we? We have all made mistakes which we were sorry for. Let's all think of this as just another lesson which has been learned. We shall be proud of the person who returns the fifty cents. We shall not blame him for his mistake. Come, bring it to me."

There was an embarrassed shuffling of feet, but no one came forward.

"Perhaps he is not quite brave enough," said Miss Besse, "while so many are watching and listening. Put your fingers in your ears, children, and put your foreheads on your desks with your eyes closed. Don't look and don't listen. When the money has been returned I'll open the windows wide. You will feel the cold air, and that will mean that the money is safely back and we can go on with our work."

She sat for a few minutes looking at all the heads on all the desks with all the elbows thrust out.

Then she passed along the front row touching each child and telling him to touch the one behind him until all were looking at her again.

"It has not come back," she said. "When you have rested a minute, we'll all cover our eyes and ears. Then not even I shall know who returns the money. He may open the window and after we feel the cold we'll stay as we are until we are sure he is back in his seat. . . Now I want to speak directly to the pupil who took the money. We don't know who you are. If you return the money after all of us put our heads down, we shall never know who you are. But we shall always know there was no really dishonest person in our class today. We shall be able to trust one another after this just as we have before. We shall be glad and proud to have Mrs. Galway's money to give to her to-morrow. We shall be glad and proud none of us kept fifty cents which would have helped some sick person to get well. Every fifty cents is needed. Every dime is needed. Every penny is needed. You will return the fifty cents, won't you? You will return it now, won't you? You will leave it on my desk and open the window and take your seat, won't you? Then this will be all over, and we can forget it, and do our spelling, and be ready to go out for recess . . . Now, children!"

All their heads went down. Hers went down. She waited to feel a small figure approach her. She waited until spots began to flash before her eyes. Just then she felt it. She saw no one; she heard no one; but she felt him, and she knew it was a boy.

She waited for the cold to come in from the

windows. It did not come. In his excitement, he must have forgotten the signal.

She raised her head slowly, cautiously, looking only at her neat desk top. There was a dime there. She stared at it.

"What on earth is this?" she exclaimed sharply.

Several children looked up. Their ears could not have been very tightly closed. An instant later all were facing her again, a few alarmed, others curious.

"The fifty cents has not been returned," she informed them. "But someone has put a dime here. What does that mean? It was five dimes, or two quarters or a half-dollar which was taken. Is someone trying to put back stolen money on the installment plan? Or does someone think this is a joking matter? Who put that dime on my desk?"

No answer.

"Very well," said Miss Besse, icy cold now. "Since no one will speak on request, every one will speak on order. We shall get to the bottom of this if it takes all day. We'll begin in this left hand corner and go up and down every row. Deborah Marshall, did you take fifty cents from my desk?"

"No, Miss Besse."

"Kathryn Whitcomb, did you?"

"No, Miss Besse."

"Rupert Cailler, did you?"

"Nope."

"No . . . Gail Murphy, did you?"

"No, I didn't."

At the bottom of the fourth row she came to Johnny Lee.

"Johnny Lee, did you?"

"No—"

His voice did not fall, as the others had. It hung suspended.

Miss Besse gave him a long look. He had the palms of his hands pressed against the corners of his desk and was staring at the blank space between them.

"Johnny," she said, "perhaps you have something more to tell me."

"No," he mumbled. "Well,—I didn't—take the fifty cents—"

"Did you see someone else take the fifty cents? If you did, it is your duty to tell me. For the sake of the person who did it. And for the sake of the class."

"I—didn't," Johnny managed. He blinked desperately. "I mean—I didn't see. I don't know. But I—but I—"

"You what, Johnny?"

"I put the ten cents on your desk," he said very fast. "I felt—I mean—as if—I thought if I give that, and maybe four other people had dimes they could—spare—why—why, then the—the sick people could get well and we wouldn't have to talk any—any more about it."

After a minute Miss Besse said, "I see. I see what you were thinking, Johnny. But you were mistaken. That fifty cents which was taken by someone in this class was given by someone else to help sick people get well. That fifty cents belongs to the sick people. Other money is all very well, but it is that money we must have, because it does not belong to whoever has it. When that has been returned, if any of you children wish to add to our fund from candy money—where did you get this dime, Johnny?"

"My—mother gave it to me."

"What for?"

"For—lunch."

"I see," said Miss Besse again. "Then it must be spent for lunch. It would not be honest to use it in any other way."

She dropped the dime into the cafeteria box and walked down to Johnny's desk to leave his yellow ticket there. A yellow ticket bought soup, milk, and a piece of fruit to be eaten with a box lunch brought from home.

"Peter Barker," she continued, "did you take fifty cents from my desk?"

"No, ma'am."

"Lawrence Kennicott, did you?"

When she had asked them all, they had all said no.

"I am sorry," said Miss Besse. "I am more sorry than I can say. Deborah, go for Mr. Sturtevant and ask him to come to my room."

Every child was searched; every desk, every lunchbox, every piece of clothing in the closet was searched. The third grade was not allowed to leave the building until the end of the afternoon session. They were kept separate from the other grades in the cafeteria. They were taken to the auditorium and questioned and searched again, while the room they had left was searched in their absence.

At the close of school, the money had not been found. Miss Besse gave a letter to each pupil to take home to his parents, explaining what had happened in third grade that day, and asking each parent to talk with his child that night, and to send a reply in the morning. She said no child would be readmitted to the room without this reply from his parents.

She noticed that Johnny's face was very white, but so were the faces of many of the children. She felt like a ghost herself.

That night, at supper, Johnny gave Miss Besse's letter to his mother.

She said, "What's this, for goodness' sake? More trouble?"

She read it and pushed it across the table to his father.

"Somebody in Johnny's room stole fifty cents," she told him. "Miss Besse wants us to talk with him about it."

"If a kid of mine stole money," Jack Lee growled, "I wouldn't *talk* with him about it! . . . Johnny, did you do it?"

Johnny shook his head.

"Then what makes her think you did?"

Johnny shook his head again.

"She don't," his mother said. "I don't s'pose—"

"Then what's she sending us this letter for?" his father demanded.

"Why don't you read it and find out?" his mother snapped.

"You read it, didn't you? You must know what she's driving at."

"Well, she says she's writing to all the parents—"

"What for?"

"Oh, Jack! You don't have to get so mad. I'm just as worried as you are. Miss Besse doesn't know who stole it."

"She thinks Johnny did, though."

"Well, no—"

"Then what's she writing us a letter for? That's what I want to know. What in thunder is she writing us letters about stolen money for, if she don't think Johnny stole it?"

Deirdre began to howl.

"Now look," Marge said. "You've scared the baby. I'm trying to tell you Miss Besse doesn't know who stole it. She's writing to all the parents for them to—"

Deirdre drowned out the rest of the sentence.

"Shut that kid up," roared Jack. "I'll speak as I want to in my own house, and when I want to—"

"Well, nobody can hear you," Marge said, beginning to cry.

She got up to lift the howling baby from her highchair.

"I'll take her," Johnny said quickly. "Let me take her, Mum. I'll take her in the front room. Come with Brother, Deedy. We'll go in and see the doggie and sing, like we do every night. Come, Deedy. Come."

He led her away, holding both her hands. The door closed after them.

Jack and Marge were nearly an hour threshing out the meager bits of information in Miss Besse's letter and debating as to whether she had any good reason for sending it to them. When they had calmed down, they agreed that Marge would write briefly, after the children were in bed, to say that they had talked with Johnny and were satisfied he had not taken the fifty cents.

"He's never touched a penny in his life," said his mother, "except what we've given him. I'm just as sure of that as I am that I didn't take the money. But I can see Miss Besse's side of it. She's in a bad spot."

Johnny did not hear her say this. He was in the front room with Deirdre.

When their mother went in, she found the baby asleep in the corner of the sofa, and Johnny sitting on the floor beside her. He had been crying, and his mother did not wonder. She had cried her own eyes nearly out. But that was over now.

She picked up the baby and said, "It's kind of chilly in here. I hope you didn't catch cold.

I ought to have built a little fire. You might bring up an armful of wood from the cellar, Johnny, and leave it in the box in the front hall closet, where it will be ready when I need it. Then you'd better go to bed."

His father did not speak to Johnny as he went through the kitchen with the wood. Jack thought he had said enough for one night. Maybe too much.

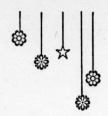

Thursday

$\mathscr{I}$T did not storm the next morning but the sky looked threatening.

Johnny was late coming down to breakfast. His mother had to call him twice. When he came she thought his face had a pinched look.

"My goodness," she said, "you look gloomy. Don't you know it's almost Christmas? Isn't it tomorrow you have your school party?"

Johnny nodded.

"I used to love Christmas parties at school," she said. "Drink your orange juice, Johnny."

He took a swallow and sat moving the glass here and there, pressing it down. It left circle marks on the red plastic table cover.

"Don't do that," his mother said. "Drink it before you spill it. Here's your cereal. We used to draw names, to give presents to. Have you drawn names?"

Johnny shook his head. He was not sure. Perhaps they had drawn names while he was in the nurse's room, sick. But he shook his head anyway.

"Well, after you get home from school, maybe we'll put Deedy on her sled and go downtown to buy a present for Miss Besse. Hurry up, Johnny. Eat."

"Mum—"

"What?"

"Could I—stay home today?"

The old refrain!

She laughed.

"Johnny Lee, we're away past that. It's almost time for school, and you're going. You couldn't stay home today of all days. You've got to take this note to Miss Besse, or she'll think you took the fifty cents."

He thought, "Linda hates Miss Besse."

He said, "Linda wasn't there yesterday."

"Maybe she's sick."

He could not imagine Linda sick. He could only imagine her inside the grotto. She was so small, as he imagined her, that she was scarcely visible. It was so long since he had seen her, to speak to her, that now it was as if she lay dead in a tiny coffin of ice which he carried in a pocket of his mind.

"Mum—"

"Johnny, I wish you'd eat. It's twenty-five

· 170 ·

minutes of nine. Remember, you've been late once this week already, and Miss Besse said—"

"Mum—"

"What, Johnny?"

"Would Dad take us up home in the truck tonight? We could—go out in the pasture and get evergreens to make wreaths."

"The idea!" his mother scoffed. "I guess your father'll be tired enough when he gets home from work without bouncing out into the country. We don't need wreaths. Johnny, you have to go. Take a big spoonful . . . There, here's the letter for Miss Besse . . . And your dime, and your lunch. Get your jacket—"

"Mum—"

"Johnny!"

"Mum, could I come home to lunch? This once?"

"Oh, Johnny, no! I've got your lunch all put up. Get your jacket! . . . Wait! Johnny!"

He stared at her, blinking.

"Johnny Lee, you've torn your sweater! Your practically new sweater! When did you do that?"

"I don' know," he mumbled.

"You do, too. When did you tear that sweater?"

"Well,—last night. I guess."

"Where? What were you doing?"

"When I—got the wood. Down cellar. On a nail."

"Oh. Down cellar. On a nail. The whole cellar to walk around in and you've got to get hung up on a nail! I declare, it's a shame. The only decent sweater you've got, practically a new one, and you not only tear it, but don't even mention it until you're ready to go, and there it is all ravelling out! I could cry!"

"I'd better," Johnny said low, "I'd better—stay home—hadn't I?"

"Stay home!" his mother exclaimed, "Stay home! Stay home! No, you will not stay home. You'll leave that sweater here, though. Come, take it off! You'll go without a sweater. You tell Miss Besse you can't go out to play. You've got to stay in because you haven't any sweater, because you tore your sweater, because it's here for me to spend an hour mending, and I don't know whether I can twotch it together or not. It's just about ruined!"

She was dragging it off over his head. She was pushing on his jacket over his shirt sleeves.

"I'll be late," Johnny whispered.

"All right. So you'll be late. You brought it on yourself. Now get there as fast as you can. And remember! You're not to go outside today until you're ready to come home! You tell Miss Besse!"

He had reached the sidewalk, running.

He called back, "Bye, Mum," over his shoulder. He could not say it very clearly.

If she answered he did not hear her. He did not think she answered.

He ran as hard as he could all the way to school. The sobs kept swelling up in his chest until it seemed as if his chest would burst. One would come out in a gust, and another was already swelling. His eyes burned, but he shed no tears. He wished he could. It seemed as if his tears had dried up from the heat inside.

The schoolground was deserted when he entered it.

The school door was closed, and it stuck. He thought he was not going to be able to open it, but at last he did. He went up the stairs and along the hall on tiptoe because it was the Rule, but panting loudly because he could not help it.

"Late again," said Miss Besse.

Johnny nodded. He hung up his jacket and left his boots. He saw that Linda was there, but she looked big and far away. She seemed like a stranger.

Miss Besse sighed.

"Why are you late again, John? Weren't you ready to start on time?"

"Yes'm."

"Then why didn't you get here on time?"

"I had to stop to take off a sweater."

"You aren't ready on time unless there is enough leeway for taking off a sweater," said Miss Besse. "If you weren't, you could have left the sweater on." But she did not press the matter that day. She asked, "Did you bring a letter from your parents?"

"Yes'm."

"Put it here with the others. After the exercises, children, you will have a study period while I read these letters."

The morning dragged. Miss Besse looked grim. She wore a dark dress with no collar. The plain silver pin at the point of the V was not quite straight. She said very little to the children. She read the letters, sighing frequently. After a while Mr. Sturtevant came in and she showed some of the letters to him. They talked in low voices, glancing darkly at the children from time to time.

Finally Miss Besse said, "Put your books away. Stand for recess."

She sounded as if it would be a relief to be rid of them.

Johnny raised his hand.

"Hands down," said Miss Besse. "No questions now. First row, get your clothes! You see, Mr. Sturtevant, Mrs. Galway may be in this noon. It seems to me—Second row! It seems to me we shall have to present the case exactly as it is. Third row! Sometimes I wonder if it is really best for collections to be made in schoolrooms, however—Fourth row!—however worthy the cause. But I don't mean that by way of excuse. Fifth row! If you can give me any advice, I'll certainly follow it. Sixth row! I admit I'm baffled. I hardly slept a wink last night . . ."

Johnny was out in the yard, with no sweater under his jacket. His mother had expressly directed him not to be there, to tell Miss Besse that he was not to be there; but Miss Besse had not allowed him to tell her that he was not to be there. He tried to think what it was best to do, when he was obliged to be where he had been ordered not to be. He thought the important thing was not to catch cold. He tried to stay out of the wind, but where there was no wind there was no sun. He jumped up and down in the shade, and swung his arms, but he could feel the cold creeping up his sleeves. He went out into the wind and the pale sunshine, and found it colder there. He decided to go back close to the building. No one seemed to notice him. He was thankful for that.

He had no trouble, except to keep warm, until the bell rang.

The ringing of the bell, the knowledge that he would soon be inside and might be able to tell Miss Besse, before noon, what his mother had said brought him a minute of something like peace.

He looked about him for the first time, saw the sun wading manfully through clouds like big gray snowdrifts, wondered if the sky over the farm looked the same, and noticed a man going down the front walk from the school building.

It was a small, elderly man, with a soft hat pulled low over his eyes. Johnny knew the man's name. It was Mr. Dwight, the new superintendent of the schools in the union. He went in and out of the building two or three times a week. Sometimes he waved his hand and smiled as he passed the third grade room. But he had not yet been inside.

The line was forming. Johnny went to find a place in it, but when he stood behind Pete, Pete lunged back into him and nearly knocked him over. He could not risk falling in the snow.

He drew back, and Kenny Schultz ran up and kicked his shins.

Johnny stood well to one side, hoping Mr. Sturtevant would not notice him. When all the others were ahead, Johnny could follow.

He watched Mr. Dwight step into his car at the end of the walk.

As he did so, something brown fell to the ground. Johnny stared, hearing the engine start.

His eyes were very keen. He could see that the object was longer than it was wide. It looked like a billfold.

The car was moving slowly, in low gear.

"Gee," Johnny whispered, "What'll I—"

The line was moving away from him. He looked for Mr. Sturtevant, but the principal, having rung the bell, had gone into the building.

"Maybe he'll turn," Johnny thought. "Maybe Mr. Dwight'll turn around at the gas station. I can give him what he dropped and be back to go in with the next grade."

He ran to the end of the walk. He could not explain to anyone what he was doing because it was the Rule that no one could speak after the bell rang. He could not shout to catch Mr. Dwight's attention because if one was not allowed to speak, surely he could not shout. But he ran as fast as he could.

The object was a billfold. It had come unsnapped as it fell and Johnny could see the edges of bills. There were a great many of them, pressed together like leaves.

He stood watching Mr. Dwight's car slowly approach the gasoline station. But it did not turn in. It began to move faster. Mr. Dwight was not going to the southern towns in the union. He was travelling north.

"Gee," Johnny whispered again, "what'll I—"

The single traffic light of the town turned red at the corner. Mr. Dwight would have to stop. Johnny had no time to lose. If he ran fast enough he would get there before the car could go through.

He doubled up his arms and ran as he had learned to run when boys were chasing him, his head down and his feet flying.

"Mr. Dwight," he kept whispering. "Mr.— Dwight—"

The last time he must have said it aloud. Mr. Dwight looked through the window of his coupé, and reached over to open the door.

"What is it, son?" he asked. "Going this way? Want a lift?"

His voice was smooth and pleasant. He had bright dark eyes.

"No," Johnny panted. "No—thanks. You dropped—this."

He laid the billfold on the seat, and closed the door.

"Wait a minute," Mr. Dwight called. "I want to speak to you. I'll just pull over to the curb out of the way."

Johnny scuttled to the sidewalk.

"Now," said Mr. Dwight, opening the door again. "Do you know what you've done for me, young man? You've prevented my losing the biggest sum of money I've carried in my pocket for a long time. I haven't opened a checking account since I came here, and I am on my way to pay the bill for a new refrigerator my wife just bought. What do you suppose she would have said to me if I had lost all that money?"

Johnny shook his head. He could not imagine that anyone would say anything very bad to a man like Mr. Dwight. He was thinking how different "young man" sounded when Mr. Dwight said it than when Mr. Sturtevant said it.

"Well, I don't know either," said Mr. Dwight. "I was very careless. But thanks to you, she can keep the new refrigerator. What's your name, son?"

Mr. Shawn had called him "son," too.

"John. Johnny Lee."

"Well, Johnny, I want to give you a reward—"

"Oh, no," Johnny said, backing away. "No. That's all right."

This was what his father would have said.

"Wait a minute," said Mr. Dwight. "I know it would be all right with you, but it wouldn't be all right with me. You see, I'll feel better if you take a reward. I might have paid around two hundred dollars for being careless. I'd feel guilty if I didn't pay a little. Here, take this for something you would like to have . . . And I'll see you again, Johnny Lee—when we can talk longer."

He nodded and smiled, and drove past the green light.

Johnny stood looking after him.

For a long time Johnny had been alone, except for Linda. Then he had been taken away from Linda. But the next day Mr. Shawn had found him, and the next morning Johnny had found God. Then, in the twinkling of an eye, God and Mr. Shawn had left him with Mrs. Curtis. Mrs. Curtis had been the best of them all; like a mother and a father and part of Linda and as much of Mr. Shawn-and-God as a small boy could be comfortable with. But he had had her for only an hour. After that, for a day and a night, he had kept a feeling of being with her, but it was only a feeling; it was not so; she, too, had gone away. Since then he had been entirely alone.

Until five minutes ago.

For five minutes he had been with Mr. Dwight.

Now he was alone again.

The wind pulled at what he held in his hand.

He looked down at the bill.

Five dollars. He had a five dollar bill.

He spread it smooth between his hands and stared at it.

Mr. Dwight had said for him to use it for something he would like to have. Five dollars was a great deal of money. But what of all that Johnny wanted would it buy?

Would it buy the farm so that he could go back and play with Linda? Would it pay his way to a part of the schoolgrounds where he could play with Linda? Would it make up for his having gone to the Baptist Church? Would it, divided, bribe Wally and Pete and Tarb and Kenny to leave him alone? Would it make him one of Mrs. Curtis' boys for good and all? Would it even help him to stand straighter and read more slowly and write more neatly and so bring him the privilege of taking books from Miss Besse's shelves?

He did not think so.

The town hall clock began striking the hour of eleven.

Johnny raised his head and looked at the clock.

He was late! He was later than he had ever been before!

Would five dollars, if he passed it to her silently, prevent Miss Besse from saying, "Late again!"? No.

He started moving woodenly toward the silent schoolgrounds. Then, suddenly, he stopped.

He was worse than late. This was much worse than being late. He had left the schoolgrounds without permission.

He could try to explain—if the words would come out—but Miss Besse did not like excuses. She would send him to Mr. Sturtevant. He could not explain to Mr. Sturtevant. If he tried, Mr. Sturtevant might not believe him. The only proof he had of where he had been was the five dollar bill. Miss Besse and Mr. Sturtevant might think he had stolen the five dollar bill. If anyone would steal fifty cents, he would steal five dollars. Mr. Sturtevant would say, "Put out your hand. Bend it back." He had not been able to make Kenny cry. But Johnny would cry. And nobody liked a boy who cried.

Johnny felt a pushing up in his chest. He did not know whether a sob was coming, or a sickness. He started running. He ran past the school and stores and up the street toward home.

Then he stopped.

He could not go home. It was not time to go home. It was a time when he was supposed to be in school. His mother would send him back. She would have to send him back. And he could not go back.

Besides, he could not explain to his mother why he had seen Mr. Dwight drop a wallet on the walk. He was not supposed to have been where he could see it. His mother had told him to stay inside that day. She had told him to tell Miss Besse that he must stay inside. And he had tried. *My mother wants me to try hard.*

He had tried, but it was like all the other times and ways he had tried. It did no good. It was no use.

He stood still.

He was all alone.

He stood there until he heard a truck which sounded like his father's truck. Then he darted down a side street and ran as hard as he could until he reached the bushes which lined the river bank. He cried there for a while, and rested. When he had stopped sobbing and panting, he went on down the river bank to the railroad bridge. It was not a very high bridge and he climbed the side of it and walked across on the tracks. He did not know where the tracks led, but he knew that when he had crossed the river he was in a different state. He remembered the tracks he had drawn for Mrs. Curtis. He had not known where they led, but she did. They went in many directions, all in search of what some boy most wanted to find out. One of them must lead to what he, Johnny, most needed to find out, though he did not know what it was. Perhaps this was the one. It was the only one he could see. He had no other choice. So he followed it.

A little way beyond the bridge, where the track curved into pine woods, he heard a train coming and stepped off into deep snow.

It was a fast train. It passed him with a thunderous roar and a rush of wind which made him shrink back. But when it had been gone a little while the strange woods seemed vast and empty. The singing of the pine needles was a ghostly sound. He shivered with cold, and wallowed through the snow back to the cleared track. Looking ahead, he saw the two black rails converging into one. He ran toward the convergence until he felt warmer, but the two rails were still separate and he was still alone, walking between them . . .

An hour later he came out of the checkerboard of dark woods and white fields, and saw ahead a cluster of houses close to the track.

He had never seen these houses before. He had never seen houses like them before. They were all small and square, all painted white with blue blinds and stone chimneys, all with a patch of lawn before them and a drying yard in the rear.

It was like a toy town.

Johnny's eyes widened.

It seemed to him that if he could leap over the intervening distance, he could kneel among these shiny little houses and move them about according to a plan of his own. He could find a little store and have it handy by for children to buy their candy in, and ice cream. The store might also sell pencils and blocks of paper. Or he might have two stores. But there would be only one church. Only one. With a bell in the steeple through which God's voice would speak to everyone; and in its vestry Mrs. Curtis would teach all the classes. If there were enough Mrs. Curtises to teach all the classes in a school, and Mr. Dwight would come to superintend it, there would be a school. Otherwise, there would be no school. The children would play all day in the fields behind the houses, and every child would do whatever he wanted to do as long as he hurt no one else. If any child hurt another, he would be put in a yard by himself until he had learned how to play without hurting. There would be Mrs. Curtises to help the children who were in yards by themselves.

Johnny knew this was a dream. Nothing real had ever been that small. There were not that many Mrs. Curtises. There was only one, and she was back in the world from which he had been driven forth, a small exile.

What he saw ahead was a real town. The nearer he came to it, the more clearly he saw that it was an outlying section of a city. Beyond the little new houses were bigger, older ones, with porches and bay windows and elm trees. Beyond the bigger houses were tall brick buildings, taller cement buildings, and many church steeples. Not one, but many.

It looked like a very great city. He wondered if this could be Detroit. Or New York. Or Washington. Texas, California, Wyoming . . .

Mrs. Curtis had said people must travel on trains or planes or by car to reach those places. She had said it would take too long to ride there on a donkey. But he had been walking a very long time, and part of the way he had been running. Other people were going there by train. They were going there faster. But he was going there too.

He had to step off the track now while another train went by. This made two trains which had passed him, filled with people riding to Detroit or Texas or Washington or whatever it was.

He began to be excited. Perhaps this was the place where he could find out what he needed to know. Perhaps even now the feast was being spread and the temple doors stood open. Perhaps wise men were waiting for boys to ask them questions.

Johnny did not return to the track. The sidewalk was comforting to his feet after the miles of ties. He looked skyward at the tallest building he could see and began to run toward it.

though he could not run fast because his feet were sore and his legs were stiff.

There were cars, trucks, and buses stopping, starting, and honking. Lights flashed at every corner. Lights ran around in circles. The sky was so dark now and there were so many lights that it might have been night. Or perhaps he was in a mighty cavern. The great buildings stood around like walls, with lights sparkling in row upon row of tiny windows.

It was beginning to snow. The air was full of big white flakes falling like silver feathers.

The sidewalk was crowded with hurrying people. None of them noticed Johnny.

He stood still and looked at them. Their faces were neither kind nor unkind. Their eyes were fixed on something farther on. They bumped into him, drew back, and hurried past in the way they had been going. His view was shut off by fur coats and paper covered packages and bulging bags.

They must all be going to the feast. The temple must be ahead.

He ran on. He tried to keep up. He stayed with the crowd.

And at last he passed through a great doorway.

He did not know what he had expected to see. Certainly not what he saw.

Immediately before him there was a long, narrow, high white table. As smooth as glass, but milk-white like marble. Behind it a white mist rose and rolled in clouds, like the smoke from a geni's arrival.

Johnny stood staring.

The mist was not only beautiful to see. It was beautiful to smell. Better than wild strawberries on the pasture hill in June. Better than garden peas and sliced cucumbers on the Fourth of July. Better than the big orange in the toe of a Christmas stocking.

Then the geni's face appeared through the mist. It was round and red, with snapping black eyes. It grinned at Johnny.

It said, "You hungry, boy?"

Hungry? . . . Everything went wavy before Johnny's eyes. He felt as if he were being taken into the beautiful mist, dissolving into it.

He could not answer, but he must have nodded, for the geni said, "Well, hop up on a stool. What'll you have? Hamburger? Hot dog? Piece of apple pie? Ice cream? Cup of hot chocolate? Coke or ginger ale?"

Hamburger . . . Hot dog . . . Piece of apple

pie . . . Ice cream . . . . Cup of hot chocolate
. . . Coke or ginger ale . . .

All the things Johnny liked best!

He saw a high, round, empty stool waiting
for him and climbed slowly onto it as if he
were being lifted. Now he and the geni were
together in the soft, warm, sweet mist.

Johnny opened his mouth.

He whispered, "I'd like—a hot dog. Please."

"A hot dog?" repeated the geni in a big, firm
voice. "I knew it. Right you are. A hot dog.
Dinner for a prince."

Dinner for a prince!

The geni turned to where a pan of frank-
fort sausages sizzled gently. He took a long
white roll from a drawer and tossed it into
the air. It somersaulted three times before he
caught it on a toasting rack.

His wide grin flashed out of the mist as he
turned his head toward Johnny.

"Mug of chocolate with the dog?" he asked.
"Warm you up."

Johnny, hunched down inside his jacket,
with his hands between his knees, was already
growing warm from the outside, but inside
there was a cold, dry channel in which it would
be wonderful to feel a hot chocolate river flow-
ing.

He nodded.

The geni touched a handle and rich liquid bubbled out.

With one sweep of his hand he placed a steaming white mug before Johnny's chin. With another he set the ruddy sausage in a golden-brown blanket beside the mug. The fragrant steam from the two combined to make a cloud which was entirely Johnny's.

Johnny said in a low voice, "I'm not a prince."

The geni gave him a quick glance which Johnny did not understand.

"Don't tell me," he said. And then, "Where's your money, bub?"

"Money?" . . . Oh, the geni knew about that five dollar bill.

"It's here," Johnny said, amazed. He took it from his inside jacket pocket.

The geni whistled.

He said, "If a boy wasn't a prince, how'd he come by that kind of money?"

"You know, don't you?" Johnny asked.

"Oh, sure," the geni grinned. "A feller gave it to you."

He took the bill. A minute later he piled up four bills, a fifty cent piece, and a quarter beside the mug.

"Put it in your pocket, Prince," he said. "Before you lose it."

He disappeared. Johnny put the money carefully into his pocket. It was bulky against his chest. He drew a long breath and began to eat.

The hot dog was the best he had ever tasted. Probably another such hot dog had never been made. He did not stop eating until he had finished it.

Once only the geni's arm and hand appeared, leaving a big smooth blob of whipped cream in the top of the mug.

Now Johnny drank. As he drank, not only was his thirst quenched, but he was warmed all through, his heart stopped pounding, his feet were no longer sore, and he began to feel happy.

"A piece of apple pie?" asked the geni, appearing. "Scoop of ice cream on it?"

Johnny nodded.

"Right you are."

The pie was there. The ice cream rode on it like a cap, melting softly and spilling over.

This was bliss.

As Johnny scraped up the last creamy drop with a spoon, the geni appeared again, his whole head and shoulders.

"What's next on your program, Prince?" he asked. "Where do you go from here?"

Johnny wiped his mouth and fingers with a paper napkin. He smiled at the geni.

"I want to stay," he said bravely. "I want to ask a man some questions."

"Right you are," the geni said. "Our Answer Man is in the next aisle. I'll call him over. Mr. Fenton!"

Johnny turned on the stool to watch him come. He was young, Johnny thought, to be an Answer Man. Not even as old as Mr. Shawn. He had no beard. His face was smooth and fair, and he had bright blue eyes like Mr. Shawn's. He wore a white shirt, like Mr. Shawn's, and a green and white necktie. A red carnation was pinned on the lapel of his dark coat.

"Mr. Fenton," the geni said, "here's a young prince who's just had a good lunch, and now he wants to ask you some questions. Where's your money, Prince?"

"Right here," Johnny smiled, touching his pocket.

"Let's see it again."

Johnny took it out and spread it on the high table.

"Look at that," the geni said. "Quite a fortune." He took one of the quarters and gave

Johnny a dime so new and shiny that it seemed never before to have been touched by human hands. "Put it away, Prince. Until you need it. Now I'll turn you over to the Answer Man."

He disappeared.

The Answer Man looked down at Johnny.

"What did you want to know?" he asked.

Johnny hardly heard what he said, he was so eager with his first question.

"Where did you get that red flower on your coat?"

"Counter One."

"Are there any more?"

"Thousands. Do you want one?"

"I want—" Johnny said. He paused. Then he said bravely, "I want three."

"This way. Follow me."

It was not far. Only a few steps, and there were red carnations in baskets and pails, on floor and counters, and on shelves reaching to the high ceiling.

From among them a girl's face smiled at the Answer Man and Johnny.

"I have a customer for you, Lorene. He wants three red carnations."

"Which ones?" Lorene asked. Her throat was white, whiter than the pearls around it.

"That one," said Johnny. "And that one. And—that one."

"Oh, my," Lorene said. "You chose the very biggest ones. They will be fifty cents."

"He has the money," the Answer Man told her. "Alex says he is a prince."

"Oh, my," Lorene said again.

Johnny took fifty cents from his pocket. Mr. Dwight had said this money was for something he wanted. He had wanted a hot dog and chocolate and pie and ice cream. Now he wanted red carnations.

"They're for my mother," he said.

"Oh, won't she be pleased! Are you going home now? Or are you going to get some other presents first?"

Johnny regarded her gravely.

"I'm not going home for a long time," he told her.

"Then why don't you let me keep the flowers in water until you're ready to go? I'll put your name on them. What is your name?"

"John. Johnny Lee."

"All right, Johnny Lee. They'll be here when you want to take them."

She had a little space between her two front teeth, like Miss Besse.

"Thank you," he said, staring up at her; and as he stared, she disappeared.

"Can I do anything else for you, Johnny?" asked the Answer Man.

"Oh, yes, sir . . . How many can I have?"

"How many what?"

"Questions."

"Quite a few. What else do you want to know?"

"Is this Detroit?"

"Detroit? . . . No. This is Treadwell. You don't live here, Johnny?"

"Oh, no, sir."

"Where do you live?"

"Very far away. Is this a temple?"

"This—no, this is—ah—an emporium."

"In an emp-orium can I find everything I need?"

"I should think so. What do you need?"

Johnny wrinkled his forehead.

"Well, there's a lot of little things. And there is a big thing that I don't know what it is. That's what I came to find out."

"What are some of the little things?"

"Well . . . One is what would make my teacher look more like—Lorene, when she looks at me. Maybe it's beads. Like the ones Lorene's got around her neck . . . And something to make Mrs.—another teacher remember me. I guess something to wear on the front of her dress. So when I look into her room I can see it on the front of her dress, and I'll know she remembered me when she put it on. You see, she can't remember me now because she's so busy with a lot of other boys . . ."

Between pauses Johnny talked faster and faster. It was easy to talk to the Answer Man because he did not interrupt, even during the pauses. He just nodded now and then, scribbling in a little book he held in the palm of his hand.

"I need a little badge to show I am a Methodist . . . And something to make four boys stop plaguing me . . . And something to give a girl that likes me—she's the only one that likes me; at school, I mean—only I don't hardly ever see her any more because I moved away and I can't go on her side of the schoolground . . . And a book to have to read at home when Miss Besse won't let me read at school. A book about—about a boy that smoked a pipe and went down river on a raft . . . And something to show my father I'm tough—like that boy was . . . And something alive for my little sister. A small animal. It would have to be a very small animal because it would have to live in the house. All she's got now to pat is the picture of a dog on a rug . . . And I need something to play music for her, too. Because she likes music. Not the radio. She likes the same piece over and over. She's little, and she'll get lonesome when it comes dark if I— if I'm not there to sing to her—"

He felt his eyes filling with tears, and blinked them back.

"Well, that's quite a list," the Answer Man said. "We'd better get started on it. Follow me."

Johnny followed him. He found that an emporium was more vast a place than he had ever imagined a temple. The ceiling seemed as high as the sky and was blue like the sky at night, with stars twinkling. He could not see the outer walls. To either side of the corridor through which he followed the Answer Man wonders were massed. Whatever there was one of there were thousands, like the carnations. Thousands of dolls. Thousands of little jars with sprigs of holly on their covers. Thousands of dishes. Thousands of Christmas wreaths. Thousands of balloons. Thousands of everything. And thousands of people looking and touching and talking and laughing.

When the Answer Man stopped, Johnny asked, "Has it always been here?"

"What?"

"The em-porium."

"No. It's new. Brand new. This is Opening Day. Lots of bargains. . . . Now here are the beads you mentioned. Pearl beads. Like Lorene's."

The treasures were given to Johnny, one after another. Pearls for Miss Besse, in white cotton, inside a little white box. A twisted gold pin for Mrs. Curtis with the words "I Love You" on it. A plain gold bar on which a machine inscribed the letters METHODIST, big and plain. Four giant chocolate bars. A picture of Johnny himself, taken by himself by pushing a button from where he sat in a brightly lit closet, looking into a mirror. A square fat book with "Tom Sawyer and Huckleberry Finn" on the cover. Two corn cob pipes with short stems; one for Johnny and one for Johnny's father.

"You won't smoke yours," said the Answer Man. "But you can chew on it, while he smokes his."

Johnny nodded.

The Answer Man was not always close beside him. Sometimes he had to go away to answer other people's questions. But he was never out of Johnny's sight, and while he was gone Johnny looked at the things in the paper bag with handles which had been given him and which had "Main Street Emporium" printed in red on the side. He looked at the white box, and the pin on the card, and the candy, and the picture of himself, and the book, and the pipes. He pinned the Methodist badge on his jacket. And all the time Lorene was keeping his mother's carnations, far more brilliant and beautiful than those which had been in the pulpit basket.

Once when the Answer man came back, Johnny looked up at him and said, "It seems as if this is a magic country. Of course it isn't. But it seems as if it is."

"It's better than that," said the Answer Man. "It's America. Now, you wanted a music box. This way."

The music box played "Lullabye and Good Night" when Johnny turned the handle.

"And a small animal. Follow me."

They went to a corner where a big yellow cat lay on a blue carpet. A small black and white kitten was cuddled against her side. A bigger, yellow kitten was lapping her ears. Two three-colored kittens were eating from a pink saucer.

"Would your little sister like one of these?"

"Oh . . . Yes, sir."

"Which one?"

"One of those eating from the saucer. The other ones are too—too little to leave their mother."

"That's right. Which one of the three-coloreds?"

"The biggest one. You have to be as big as you can—to leave your mother."

"That's right."

The geni, Alex, had kept saying "Right you are." The Answer Man kept saying, "That's right." In this place Johnny was almost always right. In other places he was almost always wrong.

"Put the biggest three-colored kitten in a box," the Answer Man told a man in a blue shirt. "Punch holes in both ends."

"You picked a beauty," said the man in the blue shirt. "You picked a beauty, my boy."

The Answer Man tucked the big box under his arm.

"That's all on our list," he said. "Except the carnations. How will you carry them all, Johnny, if you have far to go?"

"I can't carry them," Johnny said. "They will have to be sent."

"Sent where?"

"To—Mrs. John Lee, North Bainbridge, Maine."

"Then you need cards on them, don't you? Since they are for different people? Here are our gift tags. Ten in each package. And here is a desk where you can write them. I'll take the kitten down to Lorene. If you finish writing before I come back, just wait for me here."

Johnny sat in a chair which exactly fitted him. He dipped the pen in a little inkwell. He had never used a pen before.

He wrote slowly and carefully, "Miss Besse from Johnny Lee"; "Mrs. Curtis from Johnny Lee"; "Wally" and "Kenny" and "Pete" and "Tarb" from "your friend, Johnny Lee"; "Linda with love from Johnny"; "Dad from Johnny, and the other one is for me only I will not smoke it until I am older if you do not want me to but some boys do and I could"; "For my mother, to make the front room smell sweet when she plays the organ, Johnny"; and "Deedy, so you will not miss me, your big brother."

He did not make a single blot. He was sure he spelled every word right.

He did not know why writing the cards made him want to cry. It must be that any writing made him feel that way. It was a habit he must get over. He could write very nicely here in the emporium. Even Miss Besse would think so.

He wrote "John Lee, Junior" in the front of his book.

He was tying the tags to the gifts, making hard knots in the red strings, when a voice said, "Well, Johnny Lee! Hello!"

He looked up, startled. It was Mr. Dwight.

Johnny got up from his knees and smiled.

He said quickly, "Hello. See all the things I've got. You said I could use the five dollars for something I would like to have. I didn't know five dollars was so much money. You hadn't ought to give me so much. It isn't all gone. You can have some back."

He took change from his pocket and held it out.

"That's yours," Mr. Dwight said cheerfully. "I had enough to pay for the refrigerator. And I've just bought some refrigerator dishes here for my wife for Christmas. But you certainly have made a haul for less than five dollars—"

"He helped me. The Answer Man," said Johnny, pointing over Mr. Dwight's shoulder.

"It's opening day," said the Answer Man.

"That helped. Johnny, is Mr. Dwight a friend of yours?"

Johnny did not know what to say, but Mr. Dwight did.

He said briskly, "I certainly am."

"He is of mine, too, Johnny," the Answer Man said. "He was my teacher when I was your age. In fact, I guess you and I might call him a Head Answer Man."

Johnny looked at Mr. Dwight with new respect.

"Are you?" he asked. "Honest?"

"I've answered a lot of questions in my time," admitted Mr. Dwight. "The best answers usually are the ones people find for themselves. Well, Johnny, what do you say—want a ride home with all this stuff?"

Johnny was silent. Nobody else said anything.

Finally he whispered, "I wasn't going home. I was going to send them."

"I'll tell you," the Answer Man said. "I'm kind of worried about sending the kitten. She isn't used to being shut up. She's meowing quite a lot now . . . And the fact is those carnations would freeze, this weather, if they got left in a cold place. Like on a baggage truck at the station."

"My car's right outside," said Mr. Dwight. "The heater would warm it up before the cold got through to the carnations. And you could take the kitten out of the box and hold him on your lap."

"Well, couldn't you—couldn't you take take them home for me?"

"I couldn't tend the kitten and drive too. If I opened the window to signal, he might jump out. It's snowing great guns. It's getting dark. It's going to be a wild night . . . Don't you want to go home, Johnny?"

"Yes," Johnny whispered. "Yes, I—want to—"

"Then come along," said Mr. Dwight briskly.

"Follow me," said the Answer Man for the last time. But this time he put his arm around Johnny's shoulders.

Lorene gave them the flowers wrapped in paper, and the cat box. The Answer Man went as far as the car and put the cat box on Johnny's lap.

Before he closed the door, he tore a handful of sheets from his notebook and gave them to Mr. Dwight.

"It's Johnny's list of the things he needed," he said. "You and he may want to check it over. I think we got all the little things, but there was one big thing—you talk that over with the Head Answer Man, Johnny. Good-bye and good luck. Be sure to drop in at the Emporium whenever you're in Treadwell."

He waved and smiled. Mr. Dwight headed the car out into the traffic. They rode without talking until they were in the country.

Then Mr. Dwight said, "Tell me about since I saw you this morning, will you, Johnny? It must make a good story. I like to have someone tell me a story when I'm driving. It keeps me awake. How did you happen to go to Treadwell?"

The kitten was out of the box now, and Johnny had her cuddled inside his jacket, against his stomach, with only her chin sticking out. He was keeping her warm and she was keeping him warm. It was easy to talk, riding along through the stormy dark, scratching a kitten's chin.

". . . I didn't know I was going to Treadwell," he concluded. "But I had to go somewhere. I was afraid to go back to school and I was afraid to go home. Mis' Curtis said being afraid made you strong. Does it?"

"Sometimes," said Mr. Dwight. "Some people. It depends."

"Brave people, you mean?"

"Maybe they're brave. Maybe they're just the fighting kind."

"I'm not. Linda is, but I'm not . . . Does that mean I am a sissy, do you think?"

"Have you read much about Jesus, Johnny?"

"Some. And Mis' Curtis told us about him."

"Do you think he was a sissy?"

"Oh, no, sir."

"A lot of people did. Some still do. Because he said that if anybody was hit on one cheek he should turn the other."

"I think that was brave."

"It's one of the hardest things in the world to do. And I bet you've done it a lot of times."

"No. I run away."

"I didn't mean when somebody hit you with his fist. I meant when somebody was mean to you. You weren't mean back. You kept on trying to get along with him, didn't you?"

"Yes. Because I was afraid."

"Partly because you were afraid. Maybe that is how being afraid has made you strong. Without your even knowing it."

"I'm afraid to fight. Abraham Lincoln didn't like to fight. . . . But he did."

"There you are. He didn't like to. But when it was right, he did."

After a minute Johnny said, "I would fight. If it was right. If there was any chance I could beat."

"Ah," said Mr. Dwight gently. "It is a foolish man who fights when there is no chance of beating. Unless there is no other way."

"I couldn't beat Wally Stewart in a fight. Nor Bill Sudbury. Nor three or four together."

"You shouldn't have to. I couldn't fight a husky young gangster. Much less a bunch of them. I should call a policeman."

"I don't know any policeman."

"Maybe North Bainbridge needs more policemen."

"I couldn't fight Mr. Sturtevant. Nor Miss Besse. Nor—my father."

"You shouldn't have to."

"They're too big . . . And even if I could I wouldn't want to."

"No. They're your friends."

"Yes," said Johnny faintly. He added, "But they're not—not like you are."

Mr. Dwight rested his hand for an instant on Johnny's knee.

He said, "There's been a misunderstanding here. A lot of misunderstandings. Don't worry about it, Johnny. It isn't your job to straighten them out. It's mine. I'll explain to Mr. Sturtevant and Miss Besse. And to your father too. They'll understand when I explain it to them. There won't be any trouble when you get home, nor when you go back to school. I promise . . . How's the kitten?"

"She's fine," Johnny said. "Gee, she's cute."

He felt all over as his foot felt sometimes when it had been numb, and then full of hot prickles, and now was his own foot again.

"What are you going to name her?"

" . . . Lucky. They say a three-colored cat is lucky."

"This has certainly been a lucky day for both of us . . . How did you get to Treadwell, Johnny?"

"I walked."

"That was a long walk for a boy your size. Tell me about it."

Johnny told about the bushes by the river, and the bridge, and the track, and the train going by, and that reminded him of the tracks he had made on the map for Mrs. Curtis. Suddenly he laughed aloud.

He said, "When we did that at Sunday School, all the other boys knew what they wanted to find out, so we could tell where

· *209* ·

they would have to go. I didn't know what I wanted to find out, so there was no way to tell where I would have to go. But it was easy. I just got on the only track I could see, and I went to Treadwell. And then I found out."

"What did you find out, Johnny?"

"There is an emp-orium. It's even better than a temple. You can ask questions, and you can get things too. You can eat when you want to, whatever you want to eat. It tastes good. People don't scold you. They help you. It's full of wonderful things, and you can look at them all, and nobody sends you away, and you can have some of them. It seems like magic, only it's real. The Answer Man said it was better than magic; it was America . . . But North Bainbridge is in America. And there's no em-porium in North Bainbridge; is there?"

"Maybe," said Mr. Dwight. "Maybe there is. You keep on looking for it. It would be much smaller than the one in Treadwell, of course, because North Bainbridge is a much smaller town. And it would seem different to you in many ways besides size."

"Why?" Johnny asked.

He was growing sleepy.

"Because North Bainbridge is home, where

you are a small boy and people see you that
way and treat you that way. It can be a good
way, until you are older. Today you were old
enough to go to the Emporium in the big city
of Treadwell, and there you were treated as
grown-ups expect to be treated. When you are
older still, you will probably go there again,
and stay longer."

"I want," said Johnny sleepily.

"What do you want, Johnny?"

"To stay in the em-porium always when I
grow up. I want—to be an Answer Man."

"If you want to enough," said Mr. Dwight,
"you will. All in good time . . . Don't think,
though, Johnny, that life is always as you saw
it there today. Grown-ups are not always
treated as they would like to be. Life is not
often easy. But when life is hard for a child
it is harder than it could be for anyone who
has lived through the process of growing up.
What I can't see is why so few adults realize
that. They think children are happy enough
just because they are children. So when life
is hard for adults and they can't fight back
successfully at people of their own size they
often strike out at children. That's why some
children are the most miserable creatures in

the world. That's why some of them run away. That's why some of them never come back."

He knew Johnny was asleep. He was talking to himself.

In the principal's office Mr. Sturtevant had just replaced the telephone receiver on its hook.

"Well, Miss Besse," he said, "there's little news, and what we have conflicts. The boy is apparently not in the village. Mrs. Lee's husband has come from the shipyard and they are on their way here. Scouts are scouring the countryside. The crossing tender saw a boy about Johnny's size in a brown hooded jacket like Johnny's walking up the track when he went out to stop the traffic for the twelve o'clock express to go through. He shouted, but the boy gave no sign of hearing. He went on along the track out of sight. The train was a minute or two late. Nothing has been reported by the trainmen. The mailman thought he saw a boy sitting on a girder under the Forks Bridge when he drove by about eleven o'clock. He thought nothing of it at the time, but remembers it now. They couldn't both have been Johnny."

"No," agreed Miss Besse. "Funny how people always—"

"Perhaps I should try to contact the superintendent. But he is in upper towns in the union. I doubt if I could reach him."

"I wish you would try," Miss Besse said.

Mr. Sturtevant frowned. He preferred that the superintendent should not know that a boy had left his school without permission.

"I've reported to the police," he said. "Too bad we don't have a more efficient force here. They just say they never had any complaints about the boy before. I told them this was no complaint, only that the boy may be in trouble and we've got to find him. It's a cold day—"

"And it is growing dark," Miss Besse said, shivering.

"I think he'll be back when he gets hungry," Mr. Sturtevant said. "His mother says he has no money."

"I wish he had," thought Miss Besse wildly. "I wish he had stolen that fifty-cent piece we made such a fuss about. But he didn't. There it was wedged under my desk all the time. Some rascal like Kenny Schultz must have pushed it there with his toe. It never got

there by itself. If I hadn't moved the desk myself, it wouldn't have been found until next
summer. . . . If Johnny had money, I could
think maybe he had gone where he could use
money. Not into the woods . . . or into the
river . . . or under a train. But without
money—"

The young, red-headed Methodist pastor
came into the principal's office. He looked
very grave.

"I've just heard," he said, "that Johnny Lee
has disappeared. What have you found out?
What can I do? It's nearly five o'clock, and a
storm is blowing up. He had only a cotton
shirt under his jacket, because he tore his
sweater yesterday."

"Do you know Johnny?" Miss Besse asked
eagerly.

"Not as well as I wish I did."

Did anybody know Johnny?

"Last Sunday he came to our Sunday
School and . . . there was an unfortunate
incident."

"What happened?" asked Miss Besse.

"I didn't hear about it until just now. It was
our Sunday school superintendent who told me.
Since he heard of Johnny's disappearance he
just remembered that last Sunday the pulpit

· 214 ·

flowers were offered to the pupils, one blossom for each. When Johnny went up to receive his, the—well, the person in charge, who knew he had been to the Baptist Sunday school since he had been to ours, said, 'Why don't you get your flowers at the Baptist Church, young man?' So Johnny didn't take one. The superintendent thought it too bad at the time, and meant to try to explain it to Johnny, but when he looked for him again he had gone."

"Huh-huh," Mr. Sturtevant laughed, without mirth. "Well, a flower—I can't imagine a nine-year-old boy caring much whether he got a flower or not."

"Oh, I believe Johnny would like flowers," Miss Besse said. "He used to pick goldenrod on his way to school last fall."

Yes, and she had told him to leave it outside because it gave some people hay fever.

"Even if he did not want the flower," Mr. Shawn said, "perhaps it hurt him to have it refused, in such a way, when he had gone up to receive it." He looked distressed. "But hardly enough—"

"No, no," Mr. Sturtevant agreed. "Such a little thing—"

"That was Sunday," Miss Besse thought.

"Yesterday was Wednesday and I spent most of the day trying to find out who stole the fifty cents that was wedged under my desk. Tuesday I told Johnny, before the class, that he was careless. I punished him by telling him he could not have a book to read all the rest of the week, and Johnny loves to read."

She thought, "I feel skinned, as if all my nerve endings were bare. I've never felt this way before. I don't think I can stand it—"

The minister was waiting for the principal to tell him what he could do.

Mr. Sturtevant was rubbing the desk hard with the eraser of his pencil.

Then the Lees appeared silently in the doorway. Jack wore his work clothes. He was tired and tense but he had a strong grip on himself. Marge had put on her best coat, over her house dress, and tied a kerchief over her hair. Her eyes were red and swollen.

"Come in, Mrs. Lee, Mr. Lee," the principal said nervously. "Sit down. You know Mr. Shawn? And Miss Besse, Johnny's teacher?"

Jack nodded shortly. He fixed his eyes on Mr. Sturtevant.

Marge smiled faintly.

"Mr. Shawn has called," she said. "He's been real nice to Johnny." Her lips trembled.

She turned to Miss Besse. "I ought to have been to see you before," she apologized. "Johnny was always asking me to come. But I don't know. I couldn't seem to leave the baby."

"You've left her now, haven't you? And don't talk about Johnny in the past tense," Miss Besse wanted to scream.

But instead she said humbly, "I should have come to see you, Mrs. Lee. We should have talked about Johnny. We might have helped each other to help him more."

"I'm talking about him in the past tense myself," she thought.

Mr. Sturtevant looked at his watch. It showed half-past five. Jack glanced at the window. The street lights had gone on.

"I can't stop here long," he said. "I've got to get going."

Mr. Sturtevant rubbed his hands.

"Wait a minute," he said. "Let's put our heads together. How did Johnny seem to feel when he left home this morning, Mrs. Lee?"

"Same as always, I guess," Marge answered, low. "He never can eat much breakfast. He didn't want to come to school. But you told me, Mr. Sturtevant—"

"Yes," the principal answered uneasily.

"The state law requires regular attendance, of course. The school system—it's the same in all schools."

"I can't see why he felt the way he did about school," his mother said. "I always loved to go. And he said Miss Besse was nice to him."

Miss Besse's every nerve end shrieked denial.

"There are so many children in my room," she said. "What helps one may hurt another. It's hard to know. Johnny was so bright I— may have expected too much of him."

Mr. Sturtevant raised his eyebrows as if this did not make sense.

"It is a teacher's duty to see that a child's achievement is commensurate with his ability," he said. "I checked Johnny's rating on the intelligence test given him when he entered school. It was—er—very high. He should be an honor pupil. But on the report which went out just last Friday I find he had no E's, only one G, and the rest F's. Naturally, Miss Besse—"

"I knew he could get E's," Marge admitted. "His teachers always said so, but he never did. He didn't show me his card until Saturday. He was helping his father on the truck

Friday night. We moved into the village. When I saw it, I asked him why it wasn't better and he said he didn't know and asked if he could go to the movies. That made me kind of mad. I guess I was tired. I told him to stay in and write his spelling words."

That was Saturday, clicked off Miss Besse's mind.

Jack cleared his throat.

"Maybe he felt bad about leaving the farm," he said. "I found him crying in the barn two, three times last week. But I couldn't keep a farm up and carry a full-time job besides. So when I found a house in town we could get into, I sold the farm. I thought it would be better for Johnny to be where he had other kids to play with. Boys, I mean. He was by himself too much."

"The only other young one near us, out there, was Linda Morris. You know," Marge said to Miss Besse.

Miss Besse said, "I guess they were friends. Maybe Johnny missed her."

"But aren't they both in your grade?" Mr. Sturtevant asked Miss Besse.

"Yes," Miss Besse answered. "But boys and girls are separated on the playground, Mr. Sturtevant."

Mr. Sturtevant cleared his throat.

"That's true," he agreed. "Yes, certainly. It's the practice in the majority of schools."

It seemed to strengthen Mr. Sturtevant to think of how many principals did as he did, right or wrong, Johnny or no Johnny.

Mr. Shawn bent forward.

"Did he say anything about Sunday School after he got home last Sunday, Mrs. Lee?"

"No. I don't remember. Nothing special, I guess."

Jack stood up.

"I don't see as this is getting us anywhere," he said. "It's almost six o'clock. Johnny might have gone out to the farm. I'll run out there."

He crossed to the principal's desk. He bent over and spoke low but Miss Besse was near enough to hear every word.

"I'm going to get a bunch of guys to go with me. There's a lot of woods out there a little feller could get lost in if he wasn't paying attention to where he went. And the firemen've offered to . . . drag the river. I wish you'd call the police in the other towns around, and get 'em going. Wish you'd call the newspapers and the radio station—"

Miss Besse moved over beside Johnny's mother. Their shoulders touched.

"Don't you go," Miss Besse said. "Stay here with me. Everything'll be done that should be."

"I suppose I ought to go and get the baby," Marge said dully. "I left her with a neighbor I don't know very well. She isn't two years old yet, and when it begins to get dark, she cries to go home, to the farm. Johnny . . . Johnny used to comfort her."

She covered her face with her hands.

"Oh, I wish he'd worn his sweater today. I wish I'd got it mended. I wish I hadn't scolded when he tore it. It was only that he caught it on a nail in the cellar. It was a strange cellar, and he was getting me some wood, and he didn't know there was a nail—"

Miss Besse put her arm around Johnny's mother.

"He should have had an E in reading," she said. "He was the best reader in the class. That is, he read best for meaning. But I never told him so. I said the things I shouldn't have said, and didn't say the things I should have said. It's hard to do right by so many."

But excuses did not count now.

Where was Johnny?

Jack stopped by his wife.

"Don't cry, Marge," he said hoarsely.

"We'll find Johnny. You want me to take you home?"

She shook her head.

"I've got to stay here, Jack. How can I go home? I just brought the tree in from the garage this morning after Johnny left, and set out the trimmings. I was going to surprise him. I was making a wreath for the door when . . . when they called me. It's there on the kitchen table. How can I go back there? It can't be . . . it can't be Christmas without—"

"You let her stay with me, Mr. Lee," Miss Besse said quite steadily. "I'll walk up with her by-and-by. It's better for her to be here."

"But not in my room," she thought. "Not in Johnny's room. Because there is a Christmas tree there, with a paper chain that Johnny made, and paper candles pasted on the windows, and the books I wouldn't let Johnny read. Nothing else but forty empty seats—all of them Johnny's now."

As Johnny's father was going out, he met Mr. Dwight, the superintendent, coming in.

"Well, Mr. Dwight," Mr. Sturtevant said, rising. "Didn't expect to see you back today. I—er—was just going to telephone you."

Johnny's father tried to pass the superintendent, but Mr. Dwight did not move aside.

He said, "How do you do? I think you're Mr. Lee. Wait a minute, please. Why were you going to telephone me, Mr. Sturtevant?"

His voice was low and pleasant. His glance was like a firm rein which caught up everyone in the room.

Mr. Sturtevant cleared his throat.

"Mr. Lee's son—one of our third graders— left the playground at morning recess. We assumed he had gone home, but when I checked with his mother, she hadn't seen him. We haven't been able to find him. I'm just about to—er—send out an alarm to neighboring towns, and I wanted to check with you on that before I did. Of course, huh-huh, no doubt he'll turn up for supper."

"What makes you think that?"

"Well—huh—a hungry boy—"

"Perhaps Johnny has been hungry a long time. Are you Johnny's friends?"

Mr. Dwight looked at the two women.

"I'm his teacher," Miss Besse said, very low.

"I'm his . . . mother," Marge whispered.

"I see. And what have you all been doing here?"

"We were trying," Miss Besse said, "to

· 223 ·

think why Johnny would want to go away."

"And did you find reasons?"

"None," said Mr. Sturtevant, "sufficient—"

"I did," Miss Besse murmured. "I think they were quite sufficient."

Mr. Dwight regarded her approvingly.

"Those reasons must be remembered," he said. "We must try to make good use of this knowledge, if Johnny comes back to us."

"Oh, surely," Miss Besse said, "he will come back."

"Why should he?" Mr. Dwight asked.

"I don't know," Miss Besse answered. "I mean, he shouldn't. But I think he would, if he knew."

"Why do you think he would, Miss Besse?"

"Because—because children are like that!"

Mr. Dwight's eyes on Miss Besse were wholly kind.

He said gently, "I think you could be Johnny's friend."

Johnny's father said, "I've got to go. It's getting late and cold. I've got a feeling that he might be up at the farm. Maybe in the barn. He liked that barn."

"We've got a little barn where we are here," said Johnny's mother. "We thought we'd fix it into a garage to rent. But Johnny could have it, couldn't he, Jack. We could bring down some hay. He could keep rabbits—"

"I'd been thinking of a bicycle for Christmas, but we could get him a horse," his father said. "He always wanted a pony. He's too big for a pony now. But he could have a small horse."

"It's present tense again," thought Miss Besse. "Present tense for Johnny."

"When he's learned to ride," his mother said, "he can go out to Linda's whenever he wants to, on his little horse."

She stood up in her excitement and pushed back her kerchief. Her hair was short and soft.

"Oh, Jack, if you go up there, bring down something from the sitting-room. Johnny wanted that furniture. I didn't think we'd have room for it. But we will now. If we don't rent the garage. I can make it look nice, with some new cretonne. I guess he'd like that . . . Oh, if we can just find him—"

"He can't have gone far," said Mr. Sturtevant positively. "He had no money."

"Yes, he did," said Mr. Dwight quietly. "Johnny had money."

They all stared at him. He came into the room, sat on the edge of the principal's desk and smiled at them.

"Let me tell you," he said, "I am a very careless man." (*Accuracy is not enough, John. We must learn not to be careless.*) "When I left this building just as the bell was ringing at the end of recess, I dropped my billfold on the walk. Johnny saw it, and chased my car to the edge of the village to give it back to me. I had $214 in it. I saw that Johnny was a very honest boy; his jacket was unbuttoned and I saw he wore no sweater; and I saw that his eyes were sad. I made up my mind to find out more about him later. I asked his name, and I gave him five dollars as a reward . . . But I forgot there is a rule that no child is to leave the playground without permission. If I had remembered that, I should have returned with Johnny or given him a note. Because a boy with eyes like Johnny's is fearful. Such a boy has been made fearful by the very people who should have helped him to be unafraid."

But Mr. Dwight's eyes were still kind. His voice was gentle.

"So Johnny had money," he continued.

"And what," Miss Besse asked, "do you think he did after that, Mr. Dwight?"

"I think he kept on going because he did not dare come back to school and he did not

dare go home. I think he followed the railroad track because he knew it went somewhere. I think when he came to Treadwell he
spent his five dollars mostly for Christmas
presents. In fact, I know he did."

"How?" his father asked. "How do you
know, sir?"

"Because," Mr. Dwight said gently, "a former student of mine pointed him out to me in
Treadwell an hour or so ago. I gave him a
ride back here. He is outside in my car now,
with presents for his mother, father, and baby
sister, his teachers, a little girl named Linda,
and four boys whose names, he says, are
Wally, Pete, Tarb, and Kenny. He said they
weren't his friends but he wanted to be
friends with them, and he thought if he put
chocolate bars on the school tree for them
tomorrow, they might like him better. I asked
him to wait while I came in to explain to Miss
Besse and Mr. Sturtevant, and I said that
after that I would take him home and explain
to his parents. I've told him that he has nothing to fear from any of you."

"Why—er—no," said Mr. Sturtevant. "As
a matter of fact, he has missed only part of
the day: The—ah—records are all straight."

"The important record," said Mr. Dwight, "is in Johnny."

"I don't know how to thank you," Johnny's mother sobbed. "I'll—I'll write you a letter tomorrow, Mr. Dwight. But now all I can think of is—seeing Johnny."

She was already starting toward the doorway.

"Wait," Mr. Dwight said quietly. "Take time to compose yourself, Mrs. Lee. You mustn't make Johnny feel he has been the cause of any distress. Tell him just that you are here because you had begun to worry about him. He will hear later how much concern has been felt, and it will be all right then; he will know he is not blamed for it. It will help to prove to him how much people cared. But tonight just show him you are pleased that he is back, and ask about his shopping. He almost forgets to be afraid when he thinks about the presents he has bought. You will see one of those he has for you as soon as you see him, Mrs. Lee. I hope you like red carnations."

Miss Besse did not shed a tear until the Lees had gone and Mr. Shawn and Mr. Sturtevant had gone too.

Then Mr. Dwight let her cry for a while. He seemed busy at the desk.

Finally he said, "Fortunately, Miss Besse, we still have the tomorrows."

Miss Besse stood up, tucking her handkerchief inside her cuff.

"Yes, Mr. Dwight," she said.

She went downstairs. As she passed the fourth grade room, Mrs. Curtis opened the door.

"Poor Mabel!" she said. "What a day you've had! But it's come out all right, hasn't it? Mr. Shawn was just in and told me. Don't blame yourself, Mabel. It's no more your fault than everybody else's. We're all in the same boat. I had that boy in Sunday School. If I'd had my wits about me, I'd have helped you more with him this week than I have. I will after this. We'll right him around, now we've waked up. You see if we don't."

Miss Besse went on into her own room, and the Christmas tree branches were tilted up. The wreath on the door looked fat and gay. The paper candles on the windowpanes were white against the dusk.

She thought, *Tomorrow I'll praise accuracy where there isn't neatness, and neatness may follow. I'll praise neatness where there is little or no accuracy. We'll sing as long as the children want to sing. We'll all have Christmas because of Johnny. Because Johnny has given Christmas back to us.*